Report to the Commissioner

REPORT TO
THE
COMMISSIONER

by JAMES MILLS

Farrar, Straus and Giroux

NEW YORK

Quis custodiet ipsos custodes?
  —Juvenal, *Satires*

Some of the crimes we punish most vigorously cannot be found in the penal code.
   —The Hon. Ernest K. Shaplen, former
    Presiding Justice, First Department,
    New York State Appellate Division,
     commenting on the Lockley-Butler case

Acknowledgments

I am indebted to Det. Frank Batten, who first brought this report to light, and to the several other New York City detectives who read it and support its authenticity.

Preface

For weeks detectives kept telling me about Patricia Butler. I was writing a book about a Black Panther conspiracy trial, and a lot of detectives I knew came into a restaurant called Mario's across the street from the courthouse. They ate and sat around the bar and talked about the trial, and then sooner or later one of them, usually Frank Batten, was sure to turn to me and say for the hundredth time, "You know, you *really* ought to do a story about Patty Butler."

Batten was a nervous man, serious and intense. A sergeant who had ridden with him in a radio car when they got out of the police academy said everyone in the precinct wanted to work with him because he'd never take anything. If any grateful citizen started handing out cigars or whiskey, Batten took nothing. It all went to the partner.

At Mario's, Batten was a loner. Not from his own choice. The other detectives were too cautious to get friendly with him. They talked to him and drank with him, but if they wanted to gossip or discuss their cases they were careful to do it somewhere else. Batten had been in the Internal Affairs Division (IAD), and though his present assignment was the Narcotics Bureau, no one was that sure that he wasn't *still* in the IAD. Cops in the IAD are called "shoeflies" and their job, put bluntly, is to lock up other cops. They're an internal security unit, and they aren't liked. Any hint that a cop is living above his income, or sleeping with his neighbor's wife, or getting too chummy with the wrong people, and the shoeflies descend with wiretaps, tails, interviews with the friends and family. Cops want no part of anyone who is, has been, or is likely to be associated with the IAD. So they were polite to Batten, but distant.

Except when he mentioned Patty Butler. Then they fell in

with him, and no one could say enough nice things about her. They liked her because she was young and friendly and pretty, and because she was a very good detective. She was a narcotics undercover, and most of the detectives who knew her were, or had been, in the Narcotics Bureau and had seen her work. She had a lot of fans.

The assistant district attorney in charge of narcotics cases arranged for me to meet her, and later I spent a month interviewing her for a magazine. The article was never published. I am not sure why. I know the Police Department had been against it from the start, giving their authorization for Butler's cooperation only after long negotiations. Perhaps the police opposition was enough to dull the magazine's enthusiasm. Or maybe the editors read the article and just simply didn't like it. In any case, it sat in a file drawer for six months, and then one day I picked up a copy of the *Daily News* and found out she was dead. Another detective named Lockley had shot her to death in a Times Square loft, and then died himself a short time later. Two months after that, Frank Batten called me on the phone. He asked if he could meet me at Mario's.

After Butler was killed, the detective division went through a rather extensive reorganization. Harold Perna, an assistant chief inspector in charge of the Narcotics Bureau, retired under pressure, and Capt. John D'Angelo, in charge of all undercovers, was suspended. The Narcotics Bureau itself was virtually emptied out. Almost every man in it was either reassigned or retired. Batten, offered a choice between a desk job in the Commissioner's office or retirement, chose retirement. He had twenty-two years in the job, liked the work, and resented being forced out.

Batten came into Mario's carrying one of those brown cardboard legal folders that tie up with string. We sat down at a back table and after half an hour of small talk I asked him what was in the folder. He said he'd found something he wanted to give me. He said he thought that since I had written the story about Pat Butler, maybe I'd be interested in writing another story about her and the detective who killed her, and what had really happened to them. He said the whole story was in the folder. He was nervous and very formal. He handed over the folder, and then he said goodbye, very self-consciously, and shook my hand and walked out.

The folder contained six seven-inch reels of recording tape, and a stack of papers. The papers included transcripts of the tapes, plus copies of Police Department documents pertaining to the Butler homicide and the subsequent investigation. There was also a copy of my article on Butler.

I listened to the tapes, checked them against the transcripts, and decided to collect everything, almost exactly as it was handed to me, into a book. I made no deletions, changed no names. My only contribution was to dovetail the various transcribed interviews into a chronological sequence, identifying alternating speakers by name in brackets at the top of the page each time they appear. Also, I have preceded the report with a glossary of police terms that may be unfamiliar to the reader.

I have wondered, as the reader might, why Frank Batten gave me the report. Perhaps he acted out of bitterness at his forced retirement, perhaps out of affection for Pat Butler and a desire to have the story told. In any case, he voiced no restrictions and said nothing about concealing the report's source.

Glossary

A&R man   Assault and robbery specialist, a mugger

angel off   To arrest drug users emerging from a selling location, while the dealer is left temporarily undisturbed

aviator   A police superior with no steady assignment who "flies" from job to job filling in for others of his rank who are ill or on vacation

block   A group of detectives, usually four, working the same shift in the same squad

BOSS   Also, *Bossy*. Bureau of Special Services (recently redesignated Special Services Division). A unit monitoring the activities of labor groups and political organizations, often by infiltration. Other than the Narcotics Bureau, the only unit employing undercovers

chipping   Using heroin occasionally, not yet addicted

CIB   Central Intelligence Bureau. Maintains background files on known criminals

ESD   Emergency Service Division

flopped   Demoted, as from the detective division to uniformed patrolman

hook	An influential friend within the department who can be helpful in securing promotion or favored assignments
IAD	Internal Affairs Division (formerly, Police Commissioner's Confidential Investigating Unit). An internal-security unit charged with investigating complaints against police officers
KG	Known gambler, files on whom are maintained at the precinct level
MOF	Member of the force
Murphy	To pose as a pimp, collect the money in advance, and disappear without providing a girl
PC	Police Commissioner
pickup collar	An arrest (usually for a drug, morals, or gambling offense) made spontaneously, not as the result of an investigation. Pickup collars are most frequently made by plainclothesmen (patrolmen in civilian clothes), not by detectives
POSNY	People of the State of New York
pros	A prostitute
SAC	Single Agent Contact. A confidential security system introduced in the early 1960s when the Police Department began to infiltrate black officers into black political groups. Since then, the system has been employed routinely in a

variety of cases where politics or the availability of large sums of money gives cause for questioning the loyalty of an undercover. An undercover who has been "SACed" is told that his only contact with the department will be an officer meeting him at a specified address at specified times. He is led to believe that his contact's office is used for several undercovers in that area. It is assumed that if he changes sides and cooperates with the subjects of the investigation, his first act will be to betray his contact point. The individuals under investigation will then watch the contact point to determine the identities of other undercovers. In fact, the contact point is used only for that particular undercover, and if it is found to be under surveillance, the undercover is known to have been exposed

shoefly   An officer working for the IAD

Signal 13   A radio code designating an officer in need of assistance, also known as an "Assist Patrolman." The highest priority radio call. All units in the area respond

snowflake   Also, *flake*. To place incriminating evidence (drugs, betting slips, a weapon) on a suspect, as if the evidence had fallen upon him like a snowflake

swing   Days off

the Tombs   The Manhattan House of Detention for Men

toss   To search

Report to the Commissioner

The Report

POLICE DEPARTMENT
NEW YORK, N. Y. 10013

INTERNAL AFFAIRS DIVISION

This is a confidential report
prepared by the Internal Affairs
Division. Any individual not
specifically authorized in writing
by the Commissioner who examines
this report or who removes it for
any purpose from the office of
the Internal Affairs Division
will be subject to departmental
trial and-or criminal prosecution.
Do not proceed beyond this cover
sheet unless confident of your
authorization.

POLICE DEPARTMENT
NEW YORK, N. Y. 10013

INTERNAL AFFAIRS DIVISION
Oct. 4, 1971

FROM: Capt. Henry Strichter
TO: The Commissioner

SUBJ: Lockley-Butler Report, requested

　　1.　The report is divided into two sections:

　　　　A:　Routinely executed department forms
　　　　　　relating to the case.

　　　　B:　Interviews and other matter assembled
　　　　　　by this office.

　　　　　　　　　　　Respectfully submitted,

Forms

1. Unusual Occurrence Report
2. Complaint Report
3. Supplementary Complaint Report (Joseph Eagen)
4. Supplementary Complaint Report (Ballistics)
5. Arrest Report
6. Modus Operandi and Pedigree Report (front and back)

DETECTIVE DIVISION UNUSUAL OCCURRENCE REPORT

Misc. 309

DET. SQD.	DATE & DAY	TIME	PLACE OF OCCURRENCE	CRIME/CONDITION (BRIEF & CONCISE)
16	6-9-71 Wed.	1400	226 W. 47th St. (loft)	Homicide, MOF

DETAILS:

1. At time and place of occurrence a female tentatively identified as Det. Patricia Butler, shield 7310, Narcotics Bureau undercover was found DOA, victim of a homicide.

2. Investigation disclosed that at Saks Dept. Store, Fifth Ave. and 50th St., one Bo Lockley, a Third Grade Detective assigned to the 16th sqd., was in a store elevator with one Thomas Henderson, a/k/a The Stick, M/N/20, 226 W. 47th St., who he had chased there from place occurrence. Both men armed.

3. Premises evacuated, area sealed off to pedestrians and traffic.

COMPLAINANT(S)

NAME POSNY (Butler)
ADDRESS 180-73 84th Dr., Kew Gardens
SEX F RACE W AGE 22 B#
DESCRIPTION/VALUE
PROPERTY TAKEN
INJURED: YES_____ NO_____
HOSPITAL_____ CONDITION_____

NAME
ADDRESS
SEX_____ RACE_____ AGE_____ B#
DESCRIPTION/VALUE
PROPERTY TAKEN
INJURED: YES_____ NO_____
HOSPITAL_____ CONDITION_____

PERPETRATOR(S)

(IF IDENT./ARRESTED)
NAME
ADDRESS
B#
(IF NOT IDENT./ARRESTED)
SEX_____ RACE_____ AGE_____ HGT._____ WT._____
DESCRIPTION (CLOTHING)

INJURIES:

WEAPON(S)
AUTO USED: YES_____ NO_____
    PLATE/MAKE
NO. OF ARRESTS
ARRESTING OFFICER_____ CMD._____

(IF IDENT./ARRESTED)
NAME
ADDRESS
B#
(IF NOT IDENT./ARRESTED)
SEX_____ RACE_____ AGE_____ HGT._____ WT._____
DESCRIPTION (CLOTHING)

INJURIES:

WEAPON(S)
AUTO USED: YES_____ NO_____
    PLATE/MAKE
NO. OF ARRESTS
ARRESTING OFFICER_____ CMD._____

VISIT TO IDENTIFICATION UNIT YES_____ NO_____ DATE_____	SPECIAL SQUADS NOTIFIED: ESD, Ballistics Homicide

UP #1#	PCT.	CASE #	DET. ASSGND.		ALARM #
10624	16		Det. Samuel Schulman, 16th Sqd.		

DATE OF THIS REPORT	RANK AND SIGNATURE OF COMMANDING OFFICER/IN COMMAND
6-9-71	Lt. _____

COMPLAINT REPORT   (DO NOT FOLD THIS REPORT)   Duplicate Copy Required For: U.F. 61 File No. **1**

Complainant's Surname First Name Telephone No.	6. Date and Time Reported	14°	15°	19. Pct.	22. U.F. 61 No.
POSNY (Butler)	6-9-71 1400 A.M. / P.M.			16	10624

Complainant's Address Apt. No.	11. Day, Date and Time of Occurrence	16°	17°	27. Post	30. C.C.D. No.
Manhattan	6-9-71 1400 A.M. / P.M.			A2	646872

Place of Occurrence ☒ Inside ☐ Outside	38°	39°	40°	41°	42. Pct. of Arrest	43. Arrest Nos.
226 W. 47th St.					16	

Type of Premises, Business, etc.
loft

Crime or Offense (if any)
homicide

Referred to: **Dets.**
Receipt Acknowledged
Desk Officer's Signature   Rank

Received: Time / Date

Classification changed to

Precinct Commander's Signature

Rank   Name   Command

50. TYPE OF PROPERTY		51. Value of Property Stolen	57. Value of Stolen Property Recovered
1. Autos Stolen or Recovered Locally			
2. Autos Recovered by Other Auth's.			
3. Autos Recovered F. O. A.			
THIS REPORT CONCERNS: (Check One)	4. Currency		
	5. Jewelry		
Lost Property ☐	6. Furs		
	7. Clothing		
Stolen Property ☐	8. Firearms		
	9. Miscellaneous		

If an alarm is transmitted enter the following information:		
Alarm Number	Date and Time Transmitted	Property Clerk Voucher No.

Details as Reported by Complainant and/or Initial Investigating Officer.

Det. Schulman, shield 6462, 16 Sqd., report t/p/o he did find a
female, white, 22, 5-4, 115, blond, naked, half on floor half on
bed, blood xxx about front of body. Pronounced DOA by attendant
Schwarz, Roosevelt Hospital. ME Smith notified, case no. 3240.
Aided case 8840.

DESCRIPTION OF LOST OR STOLEN PROPERTY—See Appendix G of R. & P.

ARTICLE (Name only)	QUANTITY	VALUE	DESCRIPTION

DESCRIPTION OF PERSONS WANTED, PERSONS ARRESTED— See Appendix G of R. & P.

*Entries by S.R.U. only	Initial Investigating Officer's Name (Typed)	Initial Investigating Officer's Signature
	Det. Samuel Schulman 16	
	Rank Name Shield No. Command	

SUPPLEMENTARY COMPLAINT REPORT

| | | | | Duplicate Copy Required For. | | U.F. 61 File No. | 1 |

19. Pct.	Year	Det. Sqd. Ser.	Status of Case	Copy of this report forwarded to Corr. Unit for Communication.	Date of this report	22. U.F. 61 No.
16	71		Active	YES ☐ NO ☒	6-9-71	10624

DETAILS AS REPORTED BY FOLLOW UP INVESTIGATING OFFICER   Alarm Number   Is this case closed?   YES ☐   NO ☒

SUBJECT: INTERVIEW OF WITNESS JOSEPH EAGEN, M/W/27

1. The above described person, an invalid who was panhandling at the vininity of 48th St. and Sixth Ave. at approximately 1300 on 6-9-71 did observe the following persons:
   1. A Det. Lockley
   2. A M/N known as The Stick
   run East on 48th St., #1 in pursuit of #2, both with guns drawn.

2. Eagen then directed officers to an apartment at 226 W. 47 St. occupied by #2.

3. At above mentioned apartment, officers found body of W/F/22. 16th sqd. and Homicide notified.

Classification changed to		36*	39*	50. TYPE OF PROPERTY		51. Value of Property Stolen	57. Value of Stolen Property Recovered
				1. Autos Stolen or Recovered Locally			
				2. Autos Recovered by Other Auth's.			
40*	41*	42. Pct. of arrest	45. Arrest ser. no.	3. Autos Recovered F.O.A.			
				THIS REPORT CONCERNS: (Check One)	4. Currency		
					5. Jewelry		
					6. Furs		
DO NOT ENTER PROPERTY PREVIOUSLY REPORTED				Lost Property ☐	7. Clothing		
				Stolen Property ☐	8. Firearms		
					9. Miscellaneous		

DESCRIPTION OF LOST OR STOLEN PROPERTY— See Appendix G of R & P.   Property Clerk Voucher No.

ARTICLE (Name only)	QUANTITY	VALUE	DESCRIPTION

DESCRIPTIONS OF PERSONS WANTED, PERSONS ARRESTED AND ARREST DISPOSITIONS— See Appendix G of R. & P.

Investigating Officer's Name (Typed)	Investigating Officer's Signature	Commanding Officer's Signature
Det. Samuel Schulman 16	S. Schulman	
Rank Shield No. Command		

*Entries by S.R.S. only

| | | | | Duplicate Copy Required For: | | U.F. 61 File No. | 1 |

SUPPLEMENTARY COMPLAINT REPORT

19. Pct.	Year	Det. Sqd. Ser.	Status of Case	Copy of this report forwarded to Corr. Unit for Communication.	Date of this report		22. U.F. 61 No.
16	71		active	YES ☐ NO ☑	6-12-71		10624

DETAILS AS REPORTED BY FOLLOW UP INVESTIGATING OFFICER	Alarm Number	Is this case closed?
		YES ☐ NO ☑

SUBJECT: EXAMINATION BY BALLISTICS OF A .38 CAL. COLT DETS. SPEC.
SERIAL NO. 68253.

1. The aforementioned weapon delivered to ballistics by det. Schulman, 16th sqd, and said weapon showed evidence of a recent discharge.

2. Ballistics examination disclosed that this weapon was fired and contained six spent cartridges.

3. Microscopic examination of one bullet taken from the deceased disclosed that this was the weapon ~~used in the~~ ~~committed~~ commission of this crime.

4. ~~Ex~~Spent cartridges held under voucher no. 3176 (16th). Ballistics No. 2546.

Classification changed to	36*	39*	50. TYPE OF PROPERTY		51. Value of Property Stolen	57. Value of Stolen Property Recovered
			1. Autos Stolen or Recovered Locally			
			2. Autos Recovered by Other Auth's.			
40*	41*	42. Pct. of arrest	3. Autos Recovered F.O.A.			
		45. Arrest ser. no.	THIS REPORT CONCERNS: (Check One)	4. Currency		
				5. Jewelry		
				6. Furs		
			Lost Property ☐	7. Clothing		
DO NOT ENTER PROPERTY PREVIOUSLY REPORTED				8. Firearms		
			Stolen Property ☐	9. Miscellaneous		

DESCRIPTION OF LOST OR STOLEN PROPERTY— See Appendix G of R. & P.

Property Clerk Voucher No.

ARTICLE (Name only)	QUANTITY	VALUE	DESCRIPTION

DESCRIPTIONS OF PERSONS WANTED, PERSONS ARRESTED AND ARREST DISPOSITIONS— See Appendix G of R. & P.

Investigating Officer's Name (Typed)	Investigating Officer's Signature	Commanding Officer's Signature
Samuel Schulman 16	JSchulman	
Rank Shield No. Command	*Entries by S.R.S. only	

PRISONER'S SURNAME	FIRST	INITIALS	PCT.	ARREST NO.	DUPLICATE COPIES REQUIRED FOR

Lockley Bo 16 5632

ADDRESS — APT./FLOOR — DATE OF ARREST — TIME

298 Billings Pl., Massapequa, L.I. 6-10-71 1:40p

ALIAS, NICKNAME | MOTHER'S MAIDEN NAME | DATE OF BIRTH | AGE | SEX | COLOR | COMPLAINT NO. | PCT.

Perkins 9-15-48 22 M W 10624 16

PLACE OF BIRTH (City or Town, State or Country) — SOCIAL SECURITY NO.

NYC 997-56-8735

☐ MARRIED
☒ SINGLE

OCCUPATION | WHERE EMPLOYED (Company and Address)

NYPD 16th Sqd.

☒ NON-CITY RESIDENT
☐ RESIDES IN ___ PCT

☒ CITIZEN [ ] ALIEN
TYPE OF PREMISES (Business, etc.)

OCCURRENCE DATE | TIME | PLACE | ☒ INSIDE ☐ OUTSIDE | POST | SECTOR

6-9-71 2p 226W47 NYC A2 loft

COMPLAINANT'S NAME AND ADDRESS — TELEPHONE NO.

POSNY (Butler)

☒ ADVISED OF CONSTITUTIONAL RIGHTS

LICENSES/PERMITS/IDENTIFICATION CARDS (Enter Type, Serial Numbers and Disposition)

P.D. ID Card 906346

☐ FINGERPRINTED AND CHECKED FOR ACCURACY

CHARGES AND SPECIFIC OFFENSES (LIST 1, 2, 3, ETC) ☐ PICK-UP ☐ WARRANT ☒ COMPLAINT

125.00 Murder I

PHYSICAL CONDITION
☒ APPARENTLY NORMAL
☐ OTHER (DESCRIBE)

DRUG ADDICT	TYPE USED	HOW LONG	AMOUNT USED DAILY	COST
☐ YES ☐ NO				

☐ HAS FUNDS
AIDED NUMBERS

CAUSE OF ADDICTION | ☐ PREVIOUSLY ARRESTED ☐ YES | NUMBER OF TIMES | PREVIOUS TREATMENT ☐ YES ☐ NO | IF YES, DESCRIBE UNDER DETAILS

☐ MEDICAL ☐ OTHER | FOR NARCOTICS OFFENSE ☐ NO

8840

TELEPHONE CALLS (Limited to three free calls within N.Y.C.)

OTHER ARREST NUMBERS

NUMBER	NAME OF PERSON CALLED	PURPOSE	TIME

NA

PCT. PROPERTY VOUCHER NO.

EXACT LOCATION OF ARREST

Saks Dept. Store, Fifth Ave & 50th St.

PRISONER'S ADDRESS VERIFIED BY: (Rank, Name, shield, command)

Det. S. Schulman, 16 sqd.

DETAILS (Include all pertinent information not recorded above)

DATE AND TIME RECORDED
6-10-71 215p

At time and place of occurrence defendant, a police officer
(NYPD), did shoot and kill one Patricia Butler, an undercover
police officer (NYPD) with his off-duty revolver, a .38 Colt
ser. no. 68253, weapon recovered to ballistics.

RANK	ARRESTING/ASSIGNED OFFICER	TAX REGISTRY N.	SHIELD	COMMAND
LT	Seidensticker	678544		16Sqd

☒ ON DUTY
☐ OFF DUTY
☐ PLAIN CLOTHES

ARRESTED BY: ☒ OFFICER
☐ COMPLAINANT
☐ OTHER (Describe under details)

DISPOSITION OF PRISONER ☐ BAIL ☐ PERSONAL RECOGNIZANCE ☒ COURT ☐ OTHER | RANK | SIGNATURE OF DESK OFFICER

(Describe) Bellevue prison ward

ARREST REPORT

THE CITY OF NEW YORK
POLICE DEPARTMENT

PD 244-156 (9-70)

D.D. 19 (Rev. 5-57)
**MODUS OPERANDI
AND PEDIGREE REPORT**

POLICE DEPARTMENT
CITY OF NEW YORK

(Last Name) Prisoner's Name (First Name)	Date and Time of Arrest	Criminal Record No.
Lockley Bo	6-10-71 1:40 P.M.	B991684

Aliases	Nicknames	Pct. of Arrest 16	Arrest No. 5632	Standing Photo No.

Address (Include City and State or Foreign Country)	Location of Arrest Fifth Ave. & Saks Dept.Store 50thSt.	No. of Persons 1
298 Billings Pl., Massapequa, L.I.	(Rank) (Name) Arresting Officer (Shield) (Com'd) Lt. Seidensticker -- 16	

Occupation NYC Detective	Social Security No. 997-56-8735	Drug User? No	Kind of Drug Used

Crime Charged (Title and Specific Offense)
125.00 Murder I

Give concise statement of all essential details of the crime or offense

At time and plat place of occurrence did shoot and kill undercover

police officer Patricia Butler with his off-duty revolver, a Colt

serial #68253, weapon recovered.

INFORMATION FOR USE IN MODUS OPERANDI FILE

Date and Time of Crime	P.M.	ASSOCIATES ON THIS ARREST	
6-9-71	1	Name	Criminal Record No.

Crime Committed At 226 W. 47th St.	(Strike Out One) Inside Outside		

Type of Building (Vehicle, Store, Dwelling, Loft, etc.)
Loft

Entered Via (Door, Window, Roof, etc.)
--

Means of Entry (Jimmy, Key, Bodily Force)
--   NONE

Object of Crime
--

Represented Self As (Agent, Inspector, etc.)
--

Tale Told by Prisoner to Complainant   OTHER KNOWN ASSOCIATES
--   (State Names, Address and Criminal Record No.)

Vehicle Used? Describe
--   NONE

Peculiarities Committed
--

Frequents
--   IF PRISONER OWNS OR DRIVES AN AUTO, FILL IN THE
                                FOLLOWING CAPTIONS:

Complainant POSNY(Butler)	Make	Model	Year
Address Manhattan	Does Prisoner Own the Auto?	☐ Operator Lic. No. ☐ Chauffeur Lic. No.	

PERSONAL DESCRIPTION

SEX	DATE OF BIRTH	AGE	PLACE OF BIRTH	HEIGHT	WEIGHT	COLOR	COMPLEXION (CHECK ONE)	
M	9-15-48	22	NYC	6-2	180	W	☐ SALLOW ☑ FAIR ☐ LIGHT	☐ FLORID - RUDDY ☐ DARK - SWARTHY ☐ BROWN ☐ BLACK

CHECK RELEVANT MATTER BELOW

FACE:
- ☐ Round
- ☐ Square
- ☐ Narrow
- ☑ Rectangle
- ☐ Triangle Up
- ☐ Triangle Down

HAIR—COLOR:
- ☐ Black
- ☑ Brown
- ☐ Blond
- ☐ Red
- ☐ Sandy
- ☐ Gray—Mixed
- ☐ Dyed

HAIR—TYPE:
- ☐ Straight
- ☑ Curly or Wavy
- ☐ Kinky
- ☐ Partly Bald
- ☐ Bald
- ☐ Toupee

EYES—COLOR:
- ☐ Blue
- ☑ Brown
- ☐ Black
- ☐ Green or Hazel
- ☐ Maroon

EYES—TYPE:
- ☑ Large
- ☐ Small
- ☐ Deep Set
- ☐ Bulging
- ☐ Hooded Lids

EYES—DEFECTS:
- ☐ Crossed
- Blind
- ☐ Right ☐ Left
- Closed
- ☐ Right ☐ Left
- Patch Worn
- ☐ Right ☐ Left
- ☐ Glasses Worn
- Opaque Lens
- ☐ Right ☐ Left

EYES—DEFECTS
- Artificial
- ☐ Right ☐ Left
- ☐ Contact Lens
- ☐ Red—Bloodshot
- ☐ Squints—Blinks
- ☐ Each Eye of Different Color

NOSE:
- ☐ Large
- ☐ Small
- ☐ Pug
- ☑ Straight
- ☐ Pointed
- ☐ Flat
- ☐ Broken
- ☐ Convex
- ☐ Concave

MOUTH:
- ☐ Long—Wide
- ☐ Small—Narrow
- ☑ Straight Lip Line
- ☐ Full Lips
- ☐ Thin Lips
- ☐ Long Lip—Upper
- ☐ Short Lip—Upper

CHIN:
- ☑ Round
- ☐ Square
- ☐ Pointed
- ☐ Jutting
- ☐ Receding
- ☐ Cleft or Dimple
- ☐ Double Chin

EARS—TYPE:
- ☑ Large
- ☐ Small
- ☐ Flaring
- ☐ Close to Head
- ☐ Round
- ☐ Rectangle
- ☐ Triangle

EARS—DEFECTS:
- Cauliflowered
- ☐ Right ☐ Left
- Scarred
- ☐ Right ☐ Left
- Discolored
- ☐ Right ☐ Left
- Amputated
- ☐ Right ☐ Left
- Lobe Amputated
- ☐ Right ☐ Left
- Deaf
- ☐ Right ☐ Left
- ☐ Hearing Aid

EYEBROWS, BEARD
- ☐ Mustache
- ☐ Bushy Eyebrows
- ☐ Arched Eyebrows
- ☐ Meeting Eyebrows
- ☐ Beard—Heavy
- ☐ Beard—Light
- ☐ Chin Whiskers or Goatee
- ☐ Sideburns—Short
- ☐ Sideburns—Long

SCARS & MARKS—LOCATION:
- ☐ Head
- ☐ Forehead
- ☐ Face
- ☐ Neck
- Arm
- ☐ Right ☐ Left
- Hand
- ☐ Right ☐ Left
- Fingers
- ☐ Right ☐ Left
- Leg
- ☐ Right ☐ Left
- Foot
- ☐ Right ☐ Left

SCARS & MARKS—TYPE:
- ☐ Birthmarks
- ☐ Tattoos*
- ☐ Pockmarks
- ☐ Acne Marks
- ☐ Freckles
- ☐ Moles
- ☐ Warts
- ☐ Needle Marks

AMPUTATIONS AND DEFORMITIES:
- ☐ Amputations*
- ☐ Limp—Pronounced
- ☐ Limp—Slight
- ☐ Stiff Member
- ☐ Hunch Back
- ☐ Club Foot

BUILD:
- ☐ Slim
- ☑ Medium
- ☐ Heavy—Stout
- ☐ Stooped
- ☐ Round Shouldered

SPEECH:
- ☐ Gruff Voice
- ☑ Soft Voice
- ☐ Refined
- ☐ Coarse
- ☐ Effeminate
- ☐ Accent*
- ☐ Highpitched
- ☐ Lisping
- ☐ Stuttering
- ☐ Rapid Speaker
- ☐ Slow Speaker
- ☐ Mute
- ☐ Tongue Tied

PECULIARITIES:
- ☐ Left Handed
- ☐ Ambidextrous
- ☐ Twitching Features
- ☐ Sex Deviate
- ☐ Albino
- ☐ Wears Built-up Shoe
- ☐ Walks with Cane or Crutch
- ☐ Gait—Rapid
- ☐ Gait—Shuffling
- ☐ Other*

REMARKS:—*(Explain as necessary any matter checked above and include information for which no caption is provided.)

_____

_____

_____

Interviews and Other Matter

1. Det. Bo Lockley
2. Det. Richard Blackstone (Crunch)
3. Magazine article concerning Det. Butler
4. Lt. Phillip Hanson
5. CIB background on Thomas Henderson (the Stick)
6. ADA statement from Det. Lockley
7. Psychiatric evaluation of Det. Lockley
8. Observation sheet the day of Det. Lockley's death

LOCKLEY

Following is the transcription of a tape-recorded
statement taken July 5, 1971, from Det. Bo Lockley, Shield 9735, at office of Dr. J. Melton, Prison
Ward, Psychiatric Division, Bellevue Hospital, New
York, N.Y.

PRESENT: Lt. William Lyon,
Internal Affairs Division

Sgt. Lawrence Abramson,
Internal Affairs Division

Det. Bo Lockley

[LOCKLEY 1]

Q: Now, just for the record, my name is William Lyon. I am a lieutenant in the Internal Affairs Division. And you are . . .

A: (No response)

Q: Det. Lockley, I just want to get your name on the record.

A: (No response)

Q: Will you say your name, please?

A: (No response)

Q: Lockley, I know you've been through a lot, that it's been very upsetting. But you've already discussed it with other people, and the things I want to talk about are very different from the things the other detectives have asked you. We have to start somewhere, and I'd appreciate it if you'd just tell me your name. Just say it. You don't even have to look up.

A: (No response)

SGT. ABRAMSON: Look, Lockley, the lieutenant's being very nice. It won't take long, what he wants to know. There isn't anything to hide. Everyone's been very cooperative. And they're very sympathetic about you. Your father—

A: You . . . (inaudible)

LT. LYON: What? I didn't hear you.

A: (Shouting) You son of a—

Q: Lockley!

SGT. ABRAMSON: Lieutenant, he's—

(Inaudible voices. Crashing sounds. Scuffling.)

TAPE ENDS

LOCKLEY

Following is the transcription of a tape-recorded statement taken July 6, 1971, from Det. Bo Lockley, Shield 9735, at office of Dr. J. Melton, Prison Ward, Psychiatric Division, Bellevue Hospital, New York, N.Y.

PRESENT: Capt. Henry Strichter,
Internal Affairs Division

Det. Bo Lockley

[LOCKLEY 2]

Q: How are you feeling?

A: Not bad.

Q: That's one of the best I've ever seen.

A: It feels like one of the best. How's Lt. Lyon?

Q: He'll live.

A: I'm sorry about all of that. I just exploded. You know, you keep hearing the same questions over and over and over and over and over and then he started in with my father, and I had to make him stop. I felt like I had to do something to keep from flying apart.

Q: He knows that. He said he knew he was wrong the way he went at it. He's afraid the Commissioner will find out. The Commissioner is about out of patience, and when he loses his patience, the earth trembles and splits.

A: I have to admit, they didn't seem too cool.

Q: Frankly, I think the way they handled their interview was not inconsistent with other events in your recent past.

A: You sure you want that on the tape?

Q: It doesn't matter. No one will hear it or read it except me and maybe the Commissioner. So we can both be frank. It's not as if you had a career to protect. And I'm retiring in four months.

A: How do you happen to be in the IAD anyway? I wouldn't have thought that would be the sort of thing you'd like. Tailing cops, putting wires in on cops.

Q: I had a disagreement at the academy and the PC offered me this. We've been friends a long time. It was only for seven months, so I took it. And it's interesting. I've developed a taste for rotten apples. I didn't mean . . .

A: I know. It's all right. Do you miss teaching?

Q: I do. I liked meeting the kids coming in. And I enjoyed the talks we used to have. Did you go ahead with Mensa?

A: I did, and then I quit. Too many bus drivers feeding their egos on the professors, and the professors marveling at how intelligent they're making bus drivers these days. The whole thing was a little sick.

Q: I suppose so. Well, we'd better get down to it.

A: Uh-huh.

Q: I hate to repeat my colleagues, but, as Lyon said, for the record, I am Capt. Henry Strichter of the Internal Affairs Division. And your name is . . .

A: Bo Lockley, detective third grade, assigned to the 16th squad. Or anyway, I was.

Q: You know, of course, that you don't have to talk to me or answer my questions, all that. I'm sure you know all that . . .

A: I've made that speech once or twice myself. Not very often, but . . .

Q: And you are free to leave, to walk out, any time you want to.

A: Well, not exactly.

Q: I mean out of this office.

A: Yes. I understand. It's all right.

Q: And now also for the record I should say that we already know each other. Isn't that right?

A: Yes, that's right.

Q: We met . . .

A: At the police academy. You taught a class in evidence. We talked together a few times. Listen, excuse me, I don't want to interrupt, but I have to ask something.

Q: Of course.

A: Really, I mean—well, why are you here? What could you possibly have to ask? You know I've been questioned by the DA's office. I've told it all. So what . . . There isn't any . . .

Q: I know that. I know that. And I've read the statement. But this is something else. This is for the Commissioner.

A: Then what is he interested in? I've been questioned, Captain, until it's coming out my ears, and I've about had it. I think maybe I'm in just the right place, right here, and I mean, what does he want to know? What is there? I fired shots, and Butler is dead, and I've gone over it to detectives and the DA and doc-

29

tors, and what the hell does the Commissioner want from me? What does he want to *know?*

Q: Relax. Calm down. He knows there's more to this case than the superficials. This is the biggest scandal . . .

A: I've seen the papers.

Q: Well, the department is in more trouble than you are.

A: Really? Up for the rest of its natural life?

Q: No, Bo. But in a lot of trouble, believe me. People are using this, and they'll go a long way with it. The Commissioner wants to know as much as he can about what happened to you so he can reach some understanding of how you got, or how you were put, into this mess. What mistakes the department made, and why they were made. But he has to know—

A: Okay. Ask.

Q: Well, how old are you?

A: Twenty-two.

Q: That's pretty young for a detective.

A: I'm the youngest detective in the department.

Q: How did that—well, first of all, why did you join the Police Department?

A: My father—do you want to know it all? Some of it you've already heard.

Q: Yes. Just go ahead and tell it.

A: Well, my father, as you know, is a detective, and he wanted me to be a detective. And so I joined the Police Department and because . . .

Q: What's wrong?

A: I don't know. I'm just very nervous in here. Is it okay if I sit over there?

Q: Sure, go ahead.

A: Thanks.

Q: So you went into the 16th squad . . .

A: Yeah.

Q: Are you all right?

A: (No response)

Q: Do you want to stop for a while?

A: I'm just a little nervous. I've been a little scared since they put me in here. I never get any sleep in here. I've been very scared. What's going to happen to me? No one tells me. You know how detectives are, and the doctors are just as bad. My lawyer says everything's fine, that I shouldn't even be suspended, but I've heard lawyers talking to clients before. Jackson seems like a really tough guy, and I've heard about him before, and he'll bury me, I know he will, if he thinks he's got the evidence. Some of them think the grooviest thing they can do is lock up a cop. And they have to lock me up, Captain. That's what scares me so much. They *have* to lock me up. Because if they convict me and put me away then everything's fine for them. They had a bad cop, a bad apple, but he's just one out of 35,000 and we've put him away good and you shouldn't judge the department by one bad apple. But if they don't send me away, then it's like saying it wasn't my fault, and so whose fault was it? I mean when a cop kills another cop, it's *gotta* be somebody's fault, right? Every guy riding a subway with a *Daily News* in his hands knows that *everything* is *someone's* fault. So if it's not my fault, then whose is it? They can't answer that question, so they have to lock me up. And they're gonna lock me up. They're gonna do it, Captain. They're gonna lock me up. They're gonna say I took a taxi up to that flat, premeditating like hell all the way, and when I got there I shot her to death. Murder I. And if I want to cop out to manslaughter, *maybe* Jackson'll let me. But I'm gonna go away, Captain. I'm goin' away.

Q: Bo—

A: This is a creepy office. The whole place is creepy. The only thing I like about this place is that it's quiet. No one talks to anyone in here, and when they do it's in whispers. Sometimes there's an argument or a fight or something and a lot of yelling back and forth, but then it stops and it's quiet again and you don't hear anything except maybe a radio way down low or the TV. The nurses never talk to anyone. It's very quiet.

Q: It's nice sometimes, being where no one talks much.

A: Yeah, except Joey yells a lot.

Q: Who's Joey?

A: I knew him on the street. They used to pick him up a lot and send him in here for observation, and now here I am in here with him. He doesn't have any legs. He pushes himself around on a piece of wood that's nailed to two skate boards. He sells pencils on Seventh Avenue. He's real mean. Sometimes he kind of goes off and starts swearing at people and biting at

31

their ankles, and that's when they send him in here. He told me yesterday he'd been in here twenty-seven times. I got to know him on the street. He had something to do with this case. You know that. He's really got Basset's number—Doctor Melton, the chief shrink here—this is his office. Joey hates him, and I see his point. Basset is weirder than anyone in here. Joey calls him Basset because of his cheeks and his jowls. He's about sixty-five years old and they hang way down, and he never smiles, just hides in here, in his office all day. All his clothes are about a hundred sizes too big and he doesn't wear any belt or suspenders and when he does come out of the office he walks around with one hand holding his pants up like he'd just jumped up from the john. About once or twice a day he comes out of his office and just moves around the patients, sort of like he was trying to be friendly, you know, making little gestures, putting a hand on someone's shoulder or something like that, but there's just the gesture there, there's nothing behind it. Then he goes back into his office to hide some more. Joey really has his number.

Q: Tell me a little bit more about Joey.

A: He's young, about twenty-five I guess, blond, not a bad-looking guy—just no legs and a little crazy is all. He's not stupid, either. Maybe crazy, but not dumb. I think the only thing that keeps him alive in here is terrorizing Basset. He snaps at him like a dog and yanks at his pants and laughs like hell. You should hear that laugh, like a shriek. They won't let him have his skate board in here, so he just sits on his bed till someone moves him to one of the chairs by the TV, and sometimes when the chairs are all full they sit him on the floor on a pillow. One of the other patients, I mean. The nurses won't go near him because he bites them. Most of the time I do it. And that's some experience, Captain, putting your hands under the wet armpits of a legless lunatic and lugging him over and setting him down in front of a TV set like some potted plant or something. One night we all went to bed and the TV was still on and a nurse came in and turned it off and about half an hour later I heard a sound and I listened and then I went over by the TV in the dark and it was Joey sitting there crying. No one had moved him back to his bed. So I lifted him up and put him on his bed and he grabbed my hand and I thought he was going to bite it, but

I didn't pull it away and instead he kissed it. Just kissed it and let it go. Boy, I didn't get *any* sleep that night.

Q: Tell me how you happened to get into the Police Department.

A: It seems pretty strange, doesn't it. Impossible. I was never a cop. Cops are born. I went to the academy and I wore the uniform, but I was never a cop. The academy was just like school. Everything they taught was very neat and logical and understandable. And not at all like what I found when I got out on the street. That was a different world.

Q: Well, before we get into that, let's go back further. Tell me something about . . . You're from?

A: New York. I was born in New York.

Q: And your parents?

A: My mother, too. My father's from Charleston, South Carolina. His father had a restaurant there, outside the Naval Base. And when the war started, my father joined the Navy. He was stationed at the Brooklyn Navy Yard, a Boatswains Mate, and when the war ended he got a job doing something, I don't know what, at the Navy Yard there. And that was when he married my mother. And her father was a cop, and I guess he, my father, didn't like working in the Navy Yard there too much, whatever he was doing, and so he joined the PD.

Q: Where'd you live?

A: Stanton Street, the Lower East Side, until I was eight, and then we moved to Long Island, to Massapequa, I think when Dad got his gold shield.

Q: How'd you like Stanton Street? That's a rough neighborhood to grow up in.

A: Rough is right. When I was about six I was walking behind my brother who was walking with a couple of older kids, and I was just following, because the other kids were older and I didn't like them, I was afraid of them. I think they were kids we weren't supposed to play with, something like that. And they dropped back behind my brother a couple of steps and were whispering and I could hear them and they were talking about beating him up and taking something he had, some money or something, I don't know, and I heard them, and I saw some empty bottles in a doorway and I picked one up and just kept walking along holding it behind me and when they jumped my

33

brother I started swinging with the bottle. They were surprised as hell. They came off my brother and they looked at me like I was crazy or something, this little kid going at them with this bottle, and then they jumped me and they took the bottle away and beat the shit out of me until my brother came to the rescue and they got tired of pounding me and left.

Q: How old was your brother?

A: Three years older than me. Nine. And we were both really scared, because I was all bloody and we figured my father would kill us for fighting like that, and our clothes were torn and everything. So we tried to clean each other up a little, and then we went home and my father didn't do anything. I remember he just told us to change our clothes, and my mother got all upset and cried, but my father never got mad or anything. We couldn't figure it out.

I was really happy when we moved. I didn't like it there, on Stanton Street, at all. I was always getting in fights. Not getting into them really—other people were getting into fights with me. I always tried to go around people, you understand? But around there it was like a way of life, big people beat up on little people. If you weren't beating up on someone you were a sissy, there was something wrong with you. I didn't mind people thinking I was a sissy if they wanted to, I mean I didn't like them anyway whatever they thought. But all the time, everywhere I went, to school, to the store, anywhere, I was looking out for someone I'd have to fight with, just to keep from getting completely beaten up. So when we moved to Massapequa I was very happy. It was like moving into civilization. Grass and trees. And there was this kid across the street, Roger Berenson, I still remember his name, who made model airplanes. Not just model airplanes, radio-*controlled* model airplanes, big things, wing spans long as our arms, and he was only nine. I thought he was some kind of genius. We were very good friends. After the savages who infested Stanton Street, this guy was fabulous. And then later, in junior high, he got a little weird. Like in biology he was a little too eager to cut things up, you know what I mean? He'd dissect his own frog and then go around wanting to help everyone else cut up *their* frogs. He had a place in his cellar where he made radios, transmitters, everything, he called it his laboratory, and he had a lot of chemicals, not just a chemical set like

34

you get for Christmas, but professional stuff he bought some place in Brooklyn, and he'd make bombs and take them out to the beach and blow them up, and then he got into rockets and he was blasting mice up in rockets. He was the first friend I ever had. And his sister. Dumb, really dumb. Her brother got all the brains. But she was nice, and she liked me and she was fairly pretty and we got along very well. Around junior high school when Roger started getting strange with the frogs and everything, and the bombs and rockets in the cellar, I started spending more time with his sister, going to movies and things. She wasn't bad-looking, as I said, and she had this fantastic body, really an unbe*liev*able body. We started out like friends, because I was always with her brother, and then we started dating, and she really drove me wild. She found out what kind of body she had and she was torturing me with it. I went out with her, off and on, for two years, and then I remember in high school I finally made it with her, after all that time, the first girl I ever made love to.

But let's see. Right. We moved to Massapequa and I wasn't getting slaughtered any more. I had one more fight, the last fight I ever had in my life, before this thing happened. And it was over that same girl, Nancy Berenson, Roger's sister. In high school, some older kid, a senior I guess, some jerk on the football team or something like that, started insulting her. She wouldn't go out with him or neck with him or something, and one day in school, in front of me and a lot of other kids, he started telling her what great tits she had, and making faces like he was drooling over them, and he went on and on with it and he wouldn't stop, and finally I hit him. And the minute I hit him, I knew I'd made a mistake. He was bigger than I was, and lots stronger, and he kicked the shit out of me. And the important thing, the significant thing about that, was the lecture it got me from my old man. It came out of him all ready-made, like he'd had it down for years, just waiting for the chance to deliver it. All about authority, and bullies, and responsibility. I was very embarrassed, humiliated, at the beating that kid gave me, and my father sat me down and he said that to get along in the world everyone has to have some kind of muscle, some kind of power, but that responsibility is more important than power. That someone who behaves with responsibility will always come out ahead of a guy who just has muscle. And that the most powerful thing you can have is muscle *and* responsibility. And that one of the things responsibility means is never betraying the power you have, or the people who give it to you, or the people who trust you to use it properly, who depend on your using it properly to protect them or help them. So my father made me feel like I wasn't such a jerk for getting beaten up by that football guy, like I'd done the right thing in standing up against him, even though I got pounded. And I was impressed by what he said. Especially the loyalty part, the trust, not betraying. That was *very* important to my father, and I understood it and it was important to me. But it can make you tough. I mean it can make you *too* strong. A few months after I got that lecture, Tony, my dad's partner, came over to the house and they were watching TV, flipping around the channels, and on one channel some young girls, thirteen, fourteen years old, were dancing, bouncing around, very sexy, like they're making love to the television camera. And my father says, "Tell me, Tony, if you had a daughter like that, would you take her on a fishing trip or not?"

And Tony just laughed and they changed the channel. They didn't even know I was there. But I thought about it for a long time.

Q: What's a fishing trip?

A: You know, where two people go out fishing on a boat and only one comes back, and says they had an accident.

Q: A little while ago, you said you got into the job because of your father.

A: Right. He wanted me to be a detective. So I joined the department, and because he had some good hooks I got into the detective division very fast, in a couple of months.

Q: Is that all? That sounds like the short version.

A: Well, he had wanted my brother to be a detective. My brother was three years older than me. But then my brother wanted to join the Marines, and my father didn't want to fight against that, and I guess he thought that he could be a cop when he got out. But he never got out. I mean he was killed. Do you want to know about that?

Q: I want to know about everything.

A: Well, they just called and they told us Walt, my brother, was dead. I'd thought they always sent telegrams. But they

36

called. And my mother came to tell me, and her whole face was covered with fear, like she didn't know what would happen when she told me. Nothing happened. I was in his room reading, and I stayed there. Dad went out in the garden and pulled weeds. He didn't know how to act, so he just didn't act at all. No one knew what to do. Nothing that personal had happened to all of us together before. We all had dinner that night. It was terrible. No one said anything. I never knew sadness could be so embarrassing.

I stayed in Walt's room for two days, reading his books and thinking. It was as if it was my fault. As if I'd wished it, and it came true. Because it solved a problem for me, a big problem. I didn't have to worry about the Army any more, or about C.O. status, or about the absolute living hell it would be for my dad if I claimed C.O. status, or about any of the things that were scaring me about going in the Army and having to kill people. Walt had saved me from that. Mother said, "They can't take Bo now, can they?" And Dad said, "No, they can't." It was just about the only words anyone spoke for days after the phone call. I spent a long time trying to figure out the way I felt when Mother and Dad said that. I was happy. But was I happy that I didn't have to go in the Army, or was I happy that Walt had been killed and so I didn't have to go in the Army?

Q: How was he killed?

A: He was in Vietnam, and he'd been wounded, just a small wound in the hand, one of his fingers. Another man in his squad stepped on a mine and a little piece of it just took off my brother's finger. And he was lifted out with some other wounded and when they were in the air they got a call to pick up some more wounded, so they went there and when they landed, my brother jumped out of the chopper with the corpsmen to help them, and the VC opened fire and hit my brother in the head. He died in the hospital in Tokyo. Do you know that only two percent of all the wounded that make it to Tokyo die? His face was shot away and a lot of his brain. I think maybe one of the doctors in Tokyo did him a favor and killed him, or just let him die. I wouldn't feel bad about that. I think it was good, if that's what happened. So anyway, then I was a sole surviving son so I wasn't eligible for the draft. My brother saved me from the draft. He didn't save the country or South Vietnam, but he saved me. And my father wanted me to be a cop. So I joined. I figured as long as Walt had saved me from the Army, the least I could do was the next thing to it and be a cop. I knew Dad would start pushing me in that direction anyway in a while, when everyone recovered, if we ever did, and I thought I might as well volunteer without having to be pushed. I owed it to Dad and to Walt and to whatever good reasons there might have been for my going into the Army. And I figured at least it would reduce the benefits I got from Walt's being killed. But I was afraid. I thought about Dad and the way he was and what a good cop he was and the reputation he had and then I thought about being a cop like that myself and I was almost as afraid as I'd been of going in the Army. I knew I could never be like that. I didn't think it was a bad way to be, but I could never be like that.

So I joined the Police Department. I was at N.Y.U., thinking about going to law school, and instead I joined the Police Department. It was what my father wanted me to do, and what Walt would probably have wanted me to do, and to tell you the truth it was easier than arguing. I've always just preferred to do what people wanted me to do. When I was a kid I'd just sit and read and try to write poetry and stare out the window and my father would tell me to go outside and do something. I always just wanted to do what people wanted me to do and be left alone. Like at N.Y.U. my roommates were very radical, and they thought I should be radical, too. So I joined the SDS with them. I didn't care about it at all, but everyone I knew was doing it and if I didn't I would have had to spend a lot of time explaining and arguing, so I joined. It was easier, and it didn't make any difference to me. And really, strangely, it paid off, because I had thought it would hurt me in the department, having been in the SDS, but it didn't, they liked it, and they used it. When I got out of the police academy they put me right into Columbia, actually registered as a student, to try to get close to the SDS people there, and the Weathermen, but I only lasted two days. I really blew it. They had a demonstration the day after I got there, and I was in it, and they kicked me out of the school. They didn't know I was a cop. An assistant dean—

Q: Wait a minute. You're going too fast. What happened at the demonstration?

A: They wanted to get rid of the dean, and these two kids I was watching, who were supposed to be leaders, who *were* the leaders, started into the administration building. And I was with them, and we got inside and we saw about ten campus police, and we started running down the hall, through the lobby there, for this stairway, and when we got up the stairway, on the floor where the dean's office is, there was another bunch of campus cops, outside the dean's office, and they came after us and caught us. I didn't tell anyone I was a cop until that night when I went before an assistant dean and he told me I was out, expelled.

I was very upset, very embarrassed. I didn't know what to do, because I couldn't go back and tell my sergeant that I had been kicked out of Columbia, when I was supposed to be there to infiltrate the Weathermen. Like I'm supposed to infiltrate the Weathermen, and I can't even stay in the school.

So I did something I shouldn't have done. I confided in this assistant dean and told him I was a cop and explained that I wasn't supposed to tell him who I was but could he smooth things over and not kick me out. I really begged him. I told him how humiliating it would be for me to have to go and tell my sergeant what a mess I'd made. But the dean didn't believe me. He smiled at me like I was crazy. He didn't even say anything. He just smiled, like he thought I was crazy for thinking he'd be dumb enough to believe I was a cop. I guess he figured the city wasn't that bad off yet.

So that's when I got transferred into the 16th squad. I should have been flopped, but my father went to bat again.

Q: What happened when you went into the 16th?

A: It was a little—I knew I wasn't going to fit with a lot of guys in the squad, that I wasn't going to see things the way they would. I knew that. I've been very liberal, always, about politics and things like that, and I knew I wouldn't be able to hide it, and I was afraid of the trouble it'd make for me. I was worried about my partner and the other guys in the block, who they'd be and what they'd think of me. But mostly I was afraid of what my reaction would be when I saw things. I knew what those guys'd be like. Not all of them, but some. Stupid, really ignorant, calling all the blacks nigger and that sort of thing. I was really hung up about that. I thought the first time some dumb white cop slapped a black man, I didn't know what I'd do, because

39

that was one thing I felt very strongly about and if I didn't do anything I'd hate myself, but if I did I'd never be able to get along in the squad. So I was really worried about it, especially about my partners. I dreamed and thought about them and I guess I got a little too uptight about it because I used to see them, these three, like I say, big dumb Irish guys hitting everyone, and calling everyone nigger.

So the first day when I reported to the squad I walked in through that little swinging gate and there's two detectives sitting at the desks and another man, a big, really huge black man, about six foot four, maybe 250 pounds, just sitting there, and I'm wondering about what he did, and I thought he looks like an A&R man. So I go in to the squad commander's office and I report to Seidensticker, and he smiles and shakes my hand, all that, and then he takes me out to the squad room again and says, "This is your block."

And he introduces the two detectives, and then he introduces the black man, *he's* in the block too, he's a *cop* too, and I couldn't *believe* it. I was really relieved. I figured I've got it made now because no one's going to go around calling anyone nigger in front of *him*.

So Seidensticker introduces us, and right away Blackstone, the black one, starts in on me.

"*Bo*," he says, with this incredulous look on his face like he's never heard of anything so ridiculous. "For Beauregard?"

I say yes. I should have lied. It says Beauregard on my birth certificate, and that's my name, but no one ever calls me that. It was my grandfather's name, and I got stuck with it. But I never use it. I use Bo. But this black cop picks up on it. He looks up at the ceiling and he says, "Beauregard. *Beau*regard. Beau*regard.* Beaure*gard.*"

Then he gives one of those big, Negro laughs and says, "You from the South, Beauregard? You got a plantation down in Georgia somewhere? How many slaves you got, Beauregard?"

So Seidensticker is laughing, and the other two detectives are laughing, and I'm standing there like an idiot, just staring, I don't know what to say. Then one of the other detectives, Sam Schulman, looks at me and sees I'm really out of it and he feels a little sorry for me and he laughs and says to me,

"Don't worry about this nigger. His big black mouth just likes to put people on."

And Blackstone laughs and slaps Schulman on the back of the neck and says, "Hey, jew man, who you callin' nigger?"

Then everyone has a laugh and Seidensticker goes back into his office and closes the door. So then Blackstone says to me, "Beauregard, let's take a walk."

BLACKSTONE

Det. Richard Blackstone was engaged in conversation at the Topper bar, 315 W. 47th St., on July 11. Blackstone was aware that he was speaking to another police officer, but he was unaware that the officer was a member of the IAD, or that the conversation was being recorded.

PRESENT: Lt. William Lyon,
Internal Affairs Division

Det. Richard Blackstone

[BLACKSTONE 1]

A: Lockley's okay. He was just never working in the same place we were working, you know what I mean? You should have seen him the first day he came into the squad. We'd heard we were getting an undercover from Bossy, so we were looking for something a little strange. But this Lockley, he was somethin' else, man. He was standin' at the gate in long hair and jeans and T-shirt and suède jacket and his fingernails were all chewed down and he looked about sixteen. I thought he was a complainant. I thought he was some school kid who'd been Murphyed. Then he said he's a detective, and he went in to see Seidensticker, and Schulman says to me, "It's happened. They sent us a hippie." And we're just lookin' at each other, like this guy is nowhere.

But he's a nice guy. He turned out to be a nice guy. Beautiful, like the kids say—quiet, passive, but things going on inside. He never should of been a cop. He never *was* a cop. A few years ago he never would of made it through the academy. But today they look for these kids, right? They're all over these kids, they eat them up. It's like it used to be with Negroes. You got problems in Harlem? You got the motherfuckers buying guns? You gotta have Negro cops. You know, if your problem's Negroes, you gotta have Negro cops. Your problem's Mafia, you gotta have guineas. And when the problem's kids, you need kids. I'll tell you how Bo got through the academy. Drugs, demonstrations, runaways, bomb throwers—that's how he got through the academy. You need kids to fight kids. And it wasn't any secret to anyone that that's how he got put in the 16th. You take a look at Times Square, at the kids in that sewer, and you know why they put Lockley there. Someone should of told him right at the start, "Hey, man, this shit's not for you." But no one told him. He never should of got into the whole thing. He just *had* to be used. It was just a matter of time until someone made a victim out of him.

Q: Why do you think he did get into it? Why do you think he joined up in the first place?

A: His father. I think, his father. By wanting to do the right thing in the family. He wanted his father to, you know, approve of him, what he was doing. I talked to him once about his old man, for a few minutes. Because when his father and I were in the two-three together a long time ago, I remember his wife came to pick him up one day and she had a kid with her, and Lockley, Bo's old man, scooped the kid up in his arms and called him sweetheart. And that hit me, hearing that word come out of Lockley, who was a tough guy, believe me, and I didn't forget it. I asked Bo if he thought that was him, that kid. He said he didn't remember it, he was too young, but it had to be either him or his brother. He said that wasn't as unusual for his old man as I'd thought, that he was a very gentle guy at home, that he gave the kids their way a lot. I could see he really admired his old man, so I think that's maybe one reason why he came on the job. He wanted to do the right thing.

[LOCKLEY 3]

So this Detective Blackstone and I go out and he says he'll show me the precinct. We stop in a bar on 45th Street, and it's filled with pimps, Murphy men, guys like that, all black, I'm the only white guy there, and we sit down at the bar and order Scotch.

And Blackstone says to me, "You're a young kid, but you're gonna find out that we could all spend our time just sleepin' if it weren't for all these fuckin' niggers comin' down here and hustlin' and robbin' all the people just tryin' to do a day's work and have some fun."

So I look to see if he's laughing, but he's not. And I don't know if he's putting me on or not. So I don't know what to say. I don't know where to put that. I don't say anything. I just listen, and he goes on about all the fuckin' niggers a little bit more, and then we leave and we walk around and he shows me some more wrong bars and points out people on the street, bookies, and KGs, and lots of people who should have been in but weren't, and all the time I'm trying to put this guy together in my mind, but I can't. He's strange. Sometimes he talks to you in his real voice, with no accent at all, and other times he puts on this Deep-South Negro accent, dialect really, and talks like that. He's hard to figure out. I could just tell from the way he moved, and the things he was telling me, that he was probably a hell of a good detective.

All the men in the squad, just about all, had nicknames, and Blackstone's was Crunch. Well, let me tell you how he got that name. About a week later, after I first walked into the squad, I was talking to a plainclothesman from division, and he had worked in Harlem and he said he knew Crunch from up there about ten years or something ago, and he said that then about

five or six of the biggest and meanest black detectives in Harlem
had a kind of vigilante group called the Black Knights. Can
you imagine that? Cops calling themselves the Black Knights?
Isn't that ridiculous? And they used to go out, maybe three
or four at a time, in one of their own cars, and when they saw
black men on the street who looked wrong, or who they knew
were dealing, or roughing people off, or something like that,
they'd jump them. They never made any arrests, they just
pounded people into the pavement. All very personal and unof-
ficial, but everyone knew who they were and everyone knew
they were cops, and this plainclothesman, a white guy, said
they were really, really feared, because if they knew you were
doing something, they didn't even bother to snowflake you or
anything that sophisticated, they just "Hey, you," slam, slam,
slam, and that was it. Case closed.

This plainclothesman said he saw four black guys hanging
around in front of a liquor store that'd been robbed about four
times in six months or something, and he told them to move on
and they just looked through him, and he walked up to the
corner, and then he came back and told them again, and they
just kept talking to each other, so he told them again and then
he walked back up to the corner, and he said this green Buick,
not a department car, with four huge black men in it stopped
and one of them got out, he said it was Crunch, and asked
him how many times he'd told those niggers to move.

And he said three times, and Crunch said, "That's two times
too many," and he waved at the car and the other three came
out and the men in front of the store saw them and started to
run, but the Black Knights caught them, and the plainclothesman
said he never saw such a slaughter. He said in about two minutes those guys were pasted all over the pavement and the
cops just very casually got back in the Buick and drove off. So
that's Crunch.

Oh, I've got to tell you one more story about Crunch. It's
got to do with Joey, the guy in here without any legs. And this
little incident I really know about because I was in the squad
when it happened. In fact, I was catching, I answered the phone.
Someone calls, someone who works in the Orange Julius stand
on 47th Street, and he calls right to the squad and says there's
a guy without any legs out on the street swearing at people and

trying to bite them. So I repeat that to the guys in the squad, and Crunch says, "Joey. That bastard's gotta go. I had enough of his fuckin' mouth." Or words to that effect.

So Crunch and I walk over and sure enough there's a little knot of people around Joey and he's swearing and yelling like a madman and every time anyone comes near him he snaps at their ankles and sometimes he gives his skate board thing that he's on a shove and shoots off into the crowd, snapping. And the people in his way jump for cover and the others laugh like hell. So Crunch pushes through the crowd, and he's mad as hell, he really looks mean.

And Joey looks up at this big black giant bearing in on him and he cocks his head a little and gets real still, and then when Crunch gets there, Joey's head springs, like a snake, and he gets his teeth into Crunch's pants cuff and hangs on like a dog, and Crunch gives his leg a big yank all the way back and lifts Joey right off his skate board and Joey lets go and scrambles with his hands back onto the board.

Then Crunch gets behind him, where Joey can't turn around and reach him, and gives the board a kick and sends it rolling off the curb into the middle of Seventh Avenue. Joey is mad as hell and yelling and swearing and cars are honking and swerving by him, and some of the crowd is laughing and some are just watching and don't know what to do.

So Crunch walks up behind Joey in the street and gives his board another kick, and sends it rolling again. So he rolls it across Broadway, down 47th Street toward the river, Joey yelling and swearing, and in about fifteen minutes they're at the docks, and Joey is exhausted from all the yelling and trying to reach around to bite Crunch's leg, and now Crunch grabs Joey under the armpits and lifts him off the board and sets him on the sidewalk and he takes the board and throws it in the river, and walks off. I go after him and he says, "That'll keep him out of trouble for a while. By the time he gets back to Seventh Avenue he won't be biting people's legs."

So I went back and a cab driver and I fished the board out of the river and put Joey back on it. That's how I got to know Joey. The first time, I mean.

So now, I mean I'm trying to tell you what this business with Crunch was doing to my head. You see, I was ready for a brutal,

48

bigoted white cop. I was scared of him, but at least I was *ready* for him. And then instead of a big, brutal, bigoted white cop, I get a big, brutal, bigoted *black* cop. I couldn't figure him out. So I got up my courage, and one afternoon in that same bar he took me to the first day, that I told you about, the black bar, I asked him, I said, "Crunch, you're a black man—"

And right away he interrupted me. He said, "I'm not a black man. Those Panther motherfuckers are black men. I'm a Negro."

And I said, "All right. You're a Negro, and a lot of the bad guys in here are Negro, and they're here for a lot of complicated reasons. I mean if I lived in Harlem and was treated the way they're treated and everything, I'd probably be a Murphy man, too. So how can you be so disrespectful to your own people like that, calling them nigger and slapping them and things like that."

Well, you should have seen that look. He looked at me like I'd just landed from Mars. He looked at me a long time, really hard, and then he smiled and he said, "You gotta be kiddin'." And then he finished his drink and said, "Let's have a change of venue," and we left.

That's the only time we ever talked about it. I just mentioned it once more to Schulman, this other detective in the block, and he said, "That's no mystery. Look at the precinct arrest figures. Eighty-five percent of the collars are blacks. You can be around the precinct ten minutes and know that almost all the crime, all the street crime, here is black, and almost all the victims are white. So maybe Crunch just hates bad guys, and it just happens that in this case the bad guys are black, so he hates the blacks, and maybe he hates them more because they're his brothers. That's not hard to understand."

Maybe it's not, but I didn't really buy it. I guess I never really got Crunch figured out. I just accepted it.

Q: How did you get along in the squad?

A: Not at all. I didn't get along at all. The squad was so completely different from what we'd been taught in the academy. I found out that the academy had all been theory, what it was *supposed* to be like, and lots of physical preparation, judo and weapons training, and lots of lectures and classes. But the precinct, that was something else, that was the way it *was*. In the academy everything was all human relations—be very polite, very understanding, approach situations from the sociological point of view, talk things out. And I ate that up. That was the way the *new* cop, the modern cop, should be, enlightened and humanistic. In the squad, on the street, I found out that that's just horseshit. Those guys on the street *eat* social workers. They don't want to talk over *nothin'*. Like in the academy, the first thing they teach you, if you hit someone arrest him. Right? Because if you had to hit him, then he must have done something to be arrested for. But on the street, if Crunch collared *half* the people he hit he'd be living in court.

So the squad was a shock. It was absurd. Really. It was like a raft in the middle of a tidal wave, and people trying to bail. The *mobs* of complainants, thinking something could be done to help them. You know, expecting television detectives who'll run out and find the attacker and bring him to justice. Man, I saw complainants get *educated*. Burglary victims. They all wanted to know why detectives weren't over at their apartments dusting for prints. "He came in the door. He came in the window. There must be fingerprints. Get the fingerprints." They didn't believe it when you told them you needed all ten for an identification. And that anyway the burglar was probably some junkie with no address. They looked at you like you were contradicting twenty years of television.

And there was this plainclothesman everyone called the Machine. Very cool. Nothing bothered him. It was just a job. He was supposed to make arrests, so he made arrests. Every night he'd pull in two junkies, or two pros, or two degenerates, and write up the paper work and go to court. Always two. He had it figured he could make two collars, do the paper work, get them to court and bailed or dismissed, in eight hours, and that was his day. He had it down to a science. If he already had his two collars and he stepped into a triple homicide, he'd just walk over the bodies and continue on his way. Why let it upset you? Roll with it.

I was looking over the complainants' bench one night, and there's this old man sitting there, calm and patient as anything, with blood trickling down his head. He's mopping it off the side of his head with a handkerchief, and just waiting very quietly to see someone. He was a cab driver and someone had mugged him. He'd been mugged so often he knew the whole drill. He knew no one would find the mugger or get his money back, but he had to come in and report or he wouldn't get the insurance, so he came in. And he answered the questions and got back in his cab and went back to work. That squad room was like spending night after night in an emergency room without splints or bandages or anything, just a couple of doctors saying, "Yes, madam, we'll do the best we can. We'll do everything we can."

So I didn't get along too well. I couldn't see it. I mean I was all right with most of the other detectives, I guess, but I didn't get anywhere. I never even made any collars, to speak of.

Q: Why was that?

A: Because everything was backward. Everything seemed like it was upside down. Like the business with Crunch. A black man calling black men niggers. Nothing fit. It was like another world where everything was mirror images. Some woman comes in—a big, dirty woman with a really foul mouth—and she's screaming how her husband assaulted her, and she screams and screams, and she's showing everyone the bruises. Well, I'm catching and I try to put her off to family court, to get a warrant, an order of protection, and this and that, but she's having none of it.

"The *bruises!*" she's screaming. "Look at the *bruises!*" She wants the guy locked up, and she's gonna see him locked up.

So I leave her there and I go over to her house to get the guy, and you should have seen him. He's about five-foot-five, skinny, scared, a really pathetic specimen. And I don't even have to talk to him. I know this guy's been getting yelled at and pounded on by this broad for years and years and years and now *she* wants *him* locked up.

I told him to go stay in a hotel some place that night and as far as the whole thing was concerned I just couldn't find him. So I went back to the squad and told her he flew the coop, and if she ever sees him again to bring him in and we'll book him.

Now, a lot of guys would have taken that collar. Assault, right? That's what I mean by upside down. *She* should have been locked up.

Another time—can I tell you one more?—another time I catch a burglary, a young girl, about twenty-two, living in an apartment on 49th Street, an actress, she says. And I go over and she says she was out at a party till late the night before and burglars took some rings she had. The door had been jimmied. I ask her if she lives alone and she says no, with her boyfriend. What's he do? He's a bartender. Where'd she get the rings? From her husband. Divorced? Separated. Does she have any idea who the burglar might be? You bet she does. Her husband. Of course. He's been after her for a year, she says, to return the rings. He says they belonged to his mother and he wants them back.

"Well," says the girl, "he's already got the baby and I'll be damned if he'll keep those rings, and I don't give a shit *whose* mother they belonged to." So she wants me to search her husband's apartment, get her the rings back, and lock him up for burglary.

Well, the hell with that. I don't care what the law is. She's lucky he didn't burn the place down while he was at it. See what I mean? I'm supposed to collar the husband? Upside down. I wouldn't have minded locking up the girl, or maybe the bartender even, but not the husband. So I gave her a runaround and forgot it.

[BLACKSTONE 2]

Q: How'd he work out in the squad?

A: (Laughs) How'd he work out? Like he looked. Jeans and a T-shirt. He wanted everyone in the squad to like him, but he didn't know how to go about it. I think he'd led a pretty sheltered life. I think the squad was a shock to him. I think the street was a shock to him. You know, the way things are.

He caught a burglary at the Harvard Club on 44th Street and we couldn't let him go. It was the only time I saw him get worked up about anything. He really wanted to go over there—probably thought he'd run into some intellectuals. But can you see that? Hunh? This sixteen-year-old hippie walks in and tells the manager of the Harvard Club he's from the 16th squad and what are the details, please? That'd convert 'em, wouldn't it? We had to hold him down, and Henckle and Schulman went over.

And once we had this prisoner in the cage, for about four hours, some big nigger female impersonator, and Lockley is over in the corner just sittin' very quietly, and after a couple of hours the nigger gets the idea Lockley is a prisoner too, 'cause no one's been talkin' to him or anything, and from the way he looks, so the nigger starts yellin' how come he has to be in the cage and that other prisoner is sittin' out there. We didn't know what he was talking about for a minute and then we saw he meant Lockley, and what are we gonna do? We had to tell him Lockley was a detective. But, man, it hurt. That's embarrassing, man. (Laughs)

Another time, Bobby Wilson, this great big spade pimp, A&R man, everything, long sheet, he's in again, some uniformed man brought him in for trying to borrow money with a brick, and Lockley's backing up the print cards. Oh, man. (Laughs) Bo's

53

sittin' there at the typewriter across from Wilson—big, strong, built like a garbage truck—and Lockley says, very quiet and gentle, "Your name, sir?"

Wilson looks at him kind of uncertain, you know? He's not too smart, and he figures maybe it's some trick. And he says, real tough, "Wilson!" Like what's it to ya. And Lockley types that in and then he says—man, I can't tell it, it's too horrible— he says, "May I ask where you live?"

And Wilson explodes. He ex*plodes!* He jumps up and he looks at me and he yells, "What you doin', man? You know me a long time! What you doin'? Who this fuck here, man? What you tryin' do to me? Who this fuck?"

He was *pissed.* Well, I don't like prisoners callin' detectives fucks, especially not right there in the squad room, but on the other hand I had to admit he had a point. It was an honest mistake. We told him Lockley was one of us, but it took about ten minutes before he'd sit down and let Bo finish the cards.

[LOCKLEY 4]

So, as I said, I didn't get many collars, and after a few weeks the Owl says he wants to see me.

Q: The Owl?

A: That's Seidensticker, the squad commander. Oliver Seidensticker. Everyone called him the Owl because he was short and fat and had a round face like an owl, never any expression on it, just blank, all the time. So the Owl tells me my performance reports are bad, that if I don't start doing something I'm going to get flopped, that I have to pull my oar.

And I know he's right, really. I *wanted* to contribute, I really did. If I'd had a good solid case with good guys and bad guys —but I never got that, there were always fine little lines, you understand? And I never seemed to draw the lines in my head the same place the penal code drew them, and I always had to go by my head instead of the penal code. So I ended up with a very embarrassing evaluation sheet.

I explained it this way to the Owl, really trying to make him understand, and he just gave me that owl look back and said he'd give it some thought.

Well, the next day Crunch comes to me, and says he had a talk with the Owl, and that I had better come up with some collars if I want to stay in the squad, and that he would like to help me. We go to this bar, and he sits me down in a booth and orders two Scotches and he takes a very fatherly kind of attitude. Now Crunch is a big guy, and when he takes a fatherly stance almost anyone is inclined to listen. He's not just tall and heavy. He has these huge shoulders and neck and a very narrow waist, and a big rectangular face that's always laughing. *Always* laughing. If you came into the squad and said your wife had just had a baby, he'd laugh, slap you on the shoulder and say,

"That's great, man." And if you came into the squad and said your wife had just been beaten and raped on the sidewalk, he'd laugh, and slap you on the shoulder, and say, "Well, that's fun city, man."

He always wore bright shirts—pink, yellow, like that—and very tight pants with a broad leather belt, and he always had the waistband showing so he'd look less like a cop, and he carried his piece in an ankle holster. He looked more like a plainclothesman, really, than a detective. And he liked working like one, too. He made a lot of collars, pickup collars, that he should have left to the division.

So anyway, we're in this bar and he's fatherly. He says, "First of all, Beauregard—" He was the only one who called me Beauregard. Everyone else called me Bo. "First of all, Beauregard," he said, "you've *got* to realize that you can't stay in the squad if all you gonna do is answer phones and fingerprint people. You got to make collars, baby. And right now you got to make some *fast*." And now he's talking in this phony Deep South dialect of his. " 'Cause the ol' Owl ain't that fond of you anyways, and he's lookin' to get rid of you and get someone who's really active. Now, you got to admit that active is what you hasn't been."

I explained to him about how I always felt as if I was expected to arrest the wrong person. For a second I thought he was going to put a hand on my shoulder.

"Look, Beauregard," he said, "you can't walk around with your own private little penal code up there in your head. You got to use the same one as everybody else. The penal code says what's good and what's bad. It says it's bad to murder your wife and it's bad to hit people with tire irons and it's bad to stable horses in the city limits without a license. You got to understand that."

I told him I did understand, and that in most cases I agreed with the penal code, but that in certain circumstances . . .

"Listen," he says, "how about junk. Shit. Heroin. You got any special feelin's about that? Up there in Beauregard's special penal code?"

"No."

"You think your conscience could handle a junk collar?"

"Of course."

56

"You wouldn't all of a sudden see things the pusher's way and send him on home?"

"No, Crunch."

"Okay. Then this night we is gonna get ol' Beauregard a felony junk collar."

So we walk over to Seventh Avenue and 47th Street, the same corner where Crunch and Joey came to grips, and then we go up the block a few yards, toward Sixth, under the fire escape there. There's always lots of junkies there, you know, and goofball addicts, and they hang around there and Duffy Square, and now there're about three or four. So we walk all the way to Sixth, slowly, and then back, and Crunch says to me that there's something going on in a room in the Bristol Hotel, this really beat-up place filled with junkies and whores and old people who can't afford to live anywhere else.

He says he knows there's someone dealing junk from one of the rooms for the past few days and what he wants to do is watch the hotel and angel off junkies who go in to cop off the guy. And then eventually he'll hit the room.

"And if we don't find felony weight in that little room," he says to me, "you can roll ol' Crunch's fingers in the ink."

So we wait under the fire escape there and sure enough after about half an hour Crunch says to me, "You see him?"

And I say, "Where?"

"The green shirt. Crossing the street now."

Well, this guy in the green shirt, a tiny, skinny little guy with hair all flying, is aiming himself across that street in a straight line for the Bristol Hotel like he'd come out of a cannon. Really going. So he disappears into the hotel. And Crunch says, "He's a gofor. You see his buddies?"

"What buddies?"

"The two niggers under the sign over there, one taller than the other. That's very interesting. Only about three reasons why niggers'd be down here to cop."

I don't say anything. Crunch is really concentrating. I don't know what he's thinking. Then he says, sort of to himself, "Well, we'll just see what develops."

Then to me he says, "Now we'll just sort of wander real easy across Seventh here to the Square and then over to Castro there, and then back across about a half block behind the niggers and then nice and easy up about ten yards back of them, and by then the gofor should be just about back and we'll hustle all of 'em into that dark little hallway there at the shoe store and give 'em a little toss. You take the gofor. I'll handle my good brothers."

So we take the little circuit around and end up back of the black guys and here comes the gofor moving like a bastard, and he gets to them and passes the stuff and right then Crunch is all over them. I never saw him cross the ten yards between us and them. He was just next to me one second and on top of them the next.

And we moved them gently into the hallway, and no one saw anything. You know you can draw a crowd around there just by spitting on the sidewalk, but Crunch moved so smooth no one noticed anything, and there we are in the hallway.

I give the gofor a toss, but he's clean because he's already passed the stuff to the black guys, or to whichever one is going to carry the weight.

And I leave the gofor in a corner and I go over to Crunch, who is giving one hell of a toss to the big guy. Then he says to me, "He's clean," and just pats his hands over the other guy's chest a little and says, "They're both clean."

But he hasn't even searched the second guy, so I turn him aside and whisper, "Let's give him a good look, Crunch. The gofor's clean too, so he's gotta have it all."

"No," Crunch says. "They're all clean. I made a mistake."

I can't believe my ears. "But, Crunch," I say, "I *know* this guy is dirty. I want to toss him."

Now Crunch gives me one of his granite looks. He says, "I'm tellin' you. Everyone's clean. I made a mistake."

I'm really sore now. I know that guy has all the junk for all three of them, which is going to be over an eighth of an ounce, and I can see my felony collar, right there. And I'm greedy. I like Crunch's idea about hitting the hotel room, too. There might even be ounces there. I'm getting greedy now, you know? I can smell the glory. And here's this stupid Crunch calling it all off. I say, "Crunch, don't be dumb. I want to search him."

Well, he's had enough. He says, "Forget it." Then out loud so they can all hear, he says, "I got one more thing to say," and

then he turns a little and very suddenly—wham! just like that—
he lets the tall guy have a shot right in the belly. He really slugs
him. The guy bends over, grabbing his stomach, and Crunch
pulls him back up by the hair and lets him have one in the
mouth.

I'm watching this, and then I get a feeling, just a *feeling,* and
I look around and here comes the gofor with a knife and I stick
out my hand and catch it just about three inches from Crunch's
neck, and the blade goes through that fat part, you know, between the thumb and the index finger, right here, and then the
flat part hits against Crunch's back and breaks off and the gofor
lets go and runs and the rest of the knife is hanging out of my
hand.

It was very fast. It didn't hurt at all. I just shook my hand
and the knife fell out.

Now the other two are scrambling to get out of that hallway
too, and Crunch just steps aside a little and lets them out and
they go running like hell up Seventh Avenue, the tall guy still
holding his stomach.

Crunch looks at my hand and we wrap handkerchiefs around
it, and then we go to the Walgreen's there and go in the back
and the guy pours stuff on it and bandages it up.

And am I filled with questions for Crunch! We get outside
and take a walk up Seventh, and I ask him, I'm still a little
angry, plus which I'm feeling like a hero now 'cause I got
wounded, and this time it wasn't me who messed up a collar,
it was the great Crunch, and I'm feeling like I could have handled the whole thing perfectly if Crunch hadn't been there to
mess things up.

So I say to him, "Crunch, why the hell did you have to slug
that guy? And why the hell didn't you let me toss the little one?
He was dirty as hell. They passed it all to him. Didn't you know
that? Why didn't we search him? Why'd you pound that guy?"

Then Crunch stops walking—we're in the light there in front
of the Hawaii-Kai—and he turns to me and he gets this big,
happy, Crunch smile, and he says, "Why, man, 'cause he's a cop.
That's why."

"He's a cop?" I say.

We start walking again.

"I thought maybe you figured that out," Crunch says. "You

59

see, the only reason two niggers'd be down here from Harlem looking to score is if there's a panic in Harlem, which there ain't, or if the stuff in that hotel room is pure dynamite, which I doubt, but still it's a possibility, or if only one of 'em's a nigger and the other's an undercover.

"Like the short one's a stool, see, and he's settin' up the gofor and the hotel for the undercover, the tall guy. So naturally if we bust the three of them, how are we gonna cut the undercover loose without it lookin' bad, right? So we don't want to burn the undercover and we don't want to mess up whatever he's got goin' in the hotel. I mean, you don't need the collar *that* bad. And so the only thing for us to do is just sort of disengage, right? When I gave the big guy a toss I found his piece and shield in his back pocket and for me that made them all clean as a fresh shirt. And then I did him an extra little favor by makin' sure that gofor wouldn't carry any suspicions around with him and start spreading stories. The undercover'd much rather get hit than burned, I *know* that, and anyway it didn't hurt as much as it looked."

We're still just walking along, and I don't have anything to say at all.

"And I got to admit somethin' else to you, Beauregard, and listen careful to it 'cause it's important. It's important as all hell. Another reason I hit the cop, it wasn't just to put protection on him, but me, too. I got to make sure that some day that gofor's not stooling and he's gettin' leaned on good for somethin' nice and all of a sudden he remembers bein' with two black guys dirty as hell and they get tossed by a big spade cop and he's cut them all loose, just like that, and he develops that recollection into something where I made money off the niggers and that's why I walked away from it, see what I mean? Or maybe the gofor's stoolin' right now for someone and he wonders why I cut 'em all loose, and he mentions it to whoever he's stoolin' for, and then I got all kinds of trouble. I got a wire on my phone, I got guys from IAD goin' over every junk case I was ever on, and I stop altogether thinkin' about first grade. So I had to make *real* sure there wasn't anything to look like a love affair between me and those niggers. And now listen, Beauregard, 'cause the lesson is this. Nothin' is *ever* what it looks like. Always know who the players are. You got to know who the actors are. Never move till you know that. And don't just know it. *Know* it. 'Cause if you don't you're gonna get hurt. And maybe you're gonna get hurt real bad."

He looked at me, studying me, and he said, "You got to be careful."

I didn't say anything. Then he said, "Listen to me."

I said, "I am."

"You got to be careful of yourself."

He was still looking at me, like right into me. "You don't believe that."

I said, "I believe that."

"No, you don't. Sometimes you have to fight. I mean fight *back*."

He stopped then, and I didn't say anything, and it was embarrassing because it was the first time he'd ever been really serious with me and talked to me without the big Crunch smile.

Then after about half a block—by now we're up in the fifties, in the 18th—he takes my wrist and looks at my bandaged-up hand and laughs and says, "Beauregard, you might be the world's worst detective, but you've got balls. I've really gotta say you've got balls. It's too bad you couldn't take that collar 'cause you'd of probably got a citation for gettin' wounded saving my life. By the time we got finished tellin' it, you'd of saved my life."

[BLACKSTONE 3]

Bo Lockley was something, all right. He was something.

Q: I heard his father's in the job, or was.

A: Still is, in the Bronx. I knew him in the two-three a long time ago. He was a real tough piece of work. You had to be. You made a collar and the guy showed up in court without a turban around his head, they said you weren't a man. There was people up there in those days'd rather kill you than take a collar for attempted discon. Of course today they'd rather kill you, period. A cop up there, especially a white cop, had to kick the shit out of six people a day just to let 'em know he was around. Otherwise they'd go right through you. Right *through* you. About ten or twelve years ago Lockley's father killed a man. He hit a flat on 117th Street, I don't remember what for, shit or something, and he went into the closet and there was a nigger in there with a knife tried to cut him and he strangled the guy right there, with his hands, right there in the closet. Just pushed him up into the back against the suits and dresses and killed him with his hands. The nigger's old lady was hangin' off his back screamin' at him while he did it. Later she said Lockley flaked the nigger, that he'd never had a knife. But I'd say the nigger probably did. Lockley wouldn't have gone to the trouble to kill him if he hadn't jumped him. He was very unemotional like that. You don't bother him, he don't bother you. But, man, go up on him, and he was *mean*. Cold, you know what I mean? Eyes like ball bearings. I saw him kick the shit out of a nigger for five minutes once, and then spend another five minutes complainin' 'cause it ruined his shine. But you *had* to be mean. You *had* to be.

Q: Doesn't sound as if he was much like Bo.

A: No, it doesn't. But I'm not so sure. He was tough on the

62

job, because you had to be, and because he hated the guys he was up against. But at home he could of been different. You don't know. I've seen guys like tigers when they're on the street, like they're fighting for their lives and their families, but at home they're just people. That could have been Lockley's old man. Bo himself was no rough kid, that's for sure. He could take care of himself if he had to, but he wasn't looking for anything but peace. He was too nice a guy even to know what kind of dirty ball game he was in. He was naïve. Idealistic. And when you take a guy who's naïve and idealistic, and he has the balls to do what's in his head, you got trouble. You got yourself a lot of trouble.

Q: Do you know where it was that Lockley first met Butler?

A: Yeah, I know. Oh, met? No. But I know where he first saw her. I was with him, and by his reaction I'm sure he'd never seen her before. He was really impressed.

Q: Why?

A: The way she looked. We were on 47th Street, walking toward Seventh Avenue, heading back to the house, and about twenty yards from the corner, Bo stopped walking. He didn't say anything, he just stopped and was looking over at the corner. There was a group of junkies standing around there, and I thought maybe he thought he'd spotted something. Then I realized what he'd seen. This girl was standing over on the side, by the curb, sort of resting against the light post there, and she was—did you ever see Butler?

Q: No.

A: Well, she was somethin' else. No kidding, somethin' *else*. I'd seen her around a couple of times before and I didn't know she was an undercover. I just figured she was another junkie, but good-looking. Some of them are, you know, when they're just chipping, before they get strung out. She was terrific-looking—nice face, good body, long blond hair. She was standing there talking to the other junkies—I mean the junkies—and I figured there's nothing unusual, she's just waiting for a trick. But Bo is looking like some enchanted evening. He's knocked out. And I laughed. I took his arm and I said, "Come on, Beauregard."

And he brushed me off, and he asked me if I knew her. I

told him she was just some junkie whore. He said, "She's good-looking for a junkie."

I said, "Yeah, she's great-looking. Come back in a week. In a week you won't recognize her."

He said, "She looks like a nice girl."

I said, "Why don't you take her home and ask your mother to give her a bath?"

He didn't like that. He said, "Don't be so fucking smart," and he said it like he meant it, like he's pissed off at me. So I stood there with him while he's watching her. And then I started thinking maybe he's gonna do something foolish.

So I said, "Let's go, Beauregard. I wanta get back to the house."

And he stalled. I said, "You wanta give her a toss, give her a toss, but let's not stand here all night."

And then he really shot me a look, like I was suggesting he pick up a free feel, and I said, "Oh, Beauregard, buddy, come on, let's go."

And he says, "Maybe she's a runaway. Maybe we should get some ID."

Then I think, "Hey, this is getting serious." And I say, "Look, Beauregard. She's a junkie. She hasn't got ID. She's a junkie whore."

And then a couple of other junkie girls started talking to her, and they all went off up Seventh Avenue and Bo and I went back to the house.

Q: Did Lockley have a girl then, do you know?

A: Not then. At least I don't think so. I think I'd have known it if he did. We used to talk about women and kid around, and I'd put him on, being single and young and good-looking, and the long hair and all that, like he must be getting a lot of ass. I asked him once if he'd ever been in love, and he said he had, in college, and then it broke up, and—my opinion, my own opinion, I think he was getting more ass than a lot of people might have guessed. He reacted to it, when there was something around. Like Butler, when he saw her. Except that was a little different, that was really some reaction. I thought afterwards, looking back, that maybe under different conditions, you know, something could have developed there.

Q: Or did develop?

A: I've heard that, and I've read it in the papers, and if you're asking me what I think of that idea, I'm telling you it's bullshit. That he killed her because he was in love with her. That's bullshit. *I* wasn't in love with her, and I can tell you if I'd walked into that flat and seen her with that nigger mother-fucker I'd have thrown shots myself. And if she'd gotten in the way, she'd be just as dead as she is now.

Q: When did you first find out who she really was?

A: When she was killed. I left the apartment where she was killed and I went over to Saks and there was a detective there who said she was a narcotics undercover. That was some shock, just having been with her body in the apartment, and now knowing that she was a cop, and, you know, a nice-looking girl. I couldn't just dismiss it then—oh, another dead junkie, tough shit. I thought about that night when Bo went all glassy-eyed over her and wanted to check her ID, and I'd said forget it she's just some junkie whore.

TAPE ENDS

ARTICLE

On January 3, 1971, the office of the Commissioner obtained a copy of a magazine article entitled "The Undercover," concerning Det. Patricia Butler. The article was never published. A copy follows.

In dark and quiet moments Detective Butler reflects upon the likelihood of dying young. "When you never think about the future [the thoughts go], about what you'll be doing in ten years, or just what is finally to become of you—then you think that maybe it's because God simply has no future for you at all." These solemn speculations are not without foundation. After a year as an undercover narcotics agent, Butler knows all about the treachery and violence of Harlem's hallways, has felt a knife at the throat, seen the shrill eyes of a pusher who thinks he smells cop, knows the bluff it takes to wrap a belt around your bicep in a room full of junkies waiting to see you stick the needle in. It's been a dangerous, unusual life—all the more so because Detective Butler is white (a rarity for Harlem undercover agents), small (only 5'4"), and a girl.

Still in her twenties, Patricia Butler is very much a girl indeed. Long blond hair, blue eyes, a bright pretty face, miniskirts—she bubbles over with the giggly enthusiasm of a Big-Ten cheerleader, the I-love-the-world competence of a TV-ad airline hostess. New York State prisons are full of men who bet their lives she could not possibly be a cop. Undercover, Pat Butler has made more buys (averaging almost two a day), set up more felony arrests (283 in one year) than any other New York cop, male or female—ever. So there is more to pretty little Patty Butler than just all that giggly girlishness.

Patricia Butler lives in Queens with her parents, in an apartment above her father's tailor shop. It was he who first suggested she become a cop. Since a part-time job as a Woolworth's salesgirl when she was fifteen, Pat had never had a job she liked. Nor was she willing to stay with something she did not like. "I wanted a job where you didn't know everything about it after the first two months." She was a secretary for an insurance company—and complaining of boredom—when her father spotted a newspaper ad concerning a city test for entrance to the police academy. She took the test, scored high, and joined the force.

Pat's cheery girlishness, and ability to pass easily as a teenager, made her a natural for decoy work. Degenerates and thieves spend a lot of time in movie theaters, and Patricia was ordered to do the same. She learned to spot the purse snatchers, switching casually from seat to seat, hunting unwatched handbags. She sat down behind a 6'2" thief, and when he reached for a bag in the seat in front, she reached for him. He was the first thief she had tried to arrest, and when she got her arm around his neck, she knew she had done the wrong thing. "I really didn't realize how big he was—until he got up and picked me up with him." He ran for the street. Pat chased him two blocks into a subway station, onto a train, through the crowded cars, and finally got close enough to hit him with her gun butt. Staring into the revolver, he surrendered.

Pat entered the Narcotics Bureau under the impression that a young white girl was what they wanted. She was mistaken. The first words out of her new boss's mouth when he saw her coming through the door were, "Well, to begin with, you're the wrong color." Pat didn't know much about drugs, and one of the things she did not know was that more than half of New York's junkies are black and that the Narcotics Bureau had never in its history employed a white girl in undercover. Another thing she did not know was that undercover agents take great pains to be filthier and sicker-looking than the filthiest, sickest junkie. They are not pretty, cheery, and well dressed. "In the beginning they just didn't know what to do with me. They were all, you know, 'Oh, what are we going to do with *her?*'"

Finally, a young Puerto Rican detective named Benny Rodriguez thought he might be able to work with Pat on a pot set (neighborhood) where she wouldn't have to look as bad as a junkie. He asked the boss if he could try her out. "Great!" the boss said. "Take her. She's yours."

Benny told Pat to make herself as messy-looking as possible

and meet him the next morning in front of the Bronx Grand
Jury. She took out her oldest, dirtiest clothes, ripped seams,
tore off buttons, painted circles under her eyes with eye liner,
and showed up in the Bronx as ordered. She walked up to
Benny, and he didn't recognize her. "Benny," she said. "It's
me. Patty."

He looked at her, up and down. "My God, I didn't mean
that bad."

Benny had planned to leave Pat in the car during most of the
day when he was working with junkies, then let her out to join
him on the pot set after dark. When he saw her, he changed
his mind. He took her to a crowded, garbage-littered corner at
Fox Street and Brook Avenue, one of New York's worst junk
neighborhoods.

Benny talked in Spanish with Puerto Rican junkies and
pushers while Pat stood dumbly silent, trying to look sick. She
was questioning her ability ever to be accepted by these people,
whose language she did not even understand, when Benny
abruptly switched to English. "Okay, man," he said to a
pusher, "but my chick'll cop for me, it's cooler that way." He
turned to Pat. "Follow him."

She tailed the man for a block and a half, into a hallway, and
there handed over five dollars and received a small, stamp-
sized glassine bag of heroin. "I was really thrilled," she remembers, "because usually you never cop your first day out. You
know, it's just not done. Another girl was out three months
before she made her first buy. But now Benny is having a nervous breakdown because he doesn't know where this guy took
me, and he figured, 'Oh, my God, if this girl gets killed!' And
he figures he's dead too, right? Because he sent me out."

Junkies have their own language, heavy with a special slang,
the misuse of which instantly exposes the speaker as a fraud.
For weeks Pat was afraid to open her mouth. "You have to be
able to rap with them so they accept you and believe you, and
you have to be able to do it so well that if a problem comes up
you can talk your way out of it. I'd stand on the street next to
Benny and I'd listen to him sounding more like a junkie than
the junkies, and I'd say to myself, 'I'm never gonna be able
to do this. I might be able to look the part, but I'm never
gonna be able to talk it.'"

Pat listened to the junkies, and listened to Benny. "He showed me everything. He taught me confidence. I really had no fear. He kept telling me everything I would have to know when I was on the street alone, and he was always trying to impress on me how you have to talk so completely differently on the street. In the beginning I used to say nothing, I was so afraid I'd say the wrong thing, and then suddenly one day I was just out there and it just happened and I was rapping with everybody and I didn't even realize it. And in the beginning I had thought that I'd never be able to do it, to make it on the street, because it was a whole new world. I looked at myself in the mirror and I said, 'Will anybody believe I'm a junkie? Will I be able to talk like that? Will I be able to convince anybody? How am I going to be able to buy from these people?' I mean, how do you think you would react if they told you that you should go out in the street and dress like a junkie and talk like a junkie and make buys and that's what you're going to do from now on?"

Finally Benny decided he had no more to teach Patricia Butler. "He just said, 'Look, you know what's going on out here, you don't need me any more.' And he cut me loose."

Patricia Butler is one of those people who like goals, so when she graduated from the protection and tutelage of Benny Rodriguez she determined to prove that despite her sex and color she could make more buys than any other undercover agent in the office. She decided to concentrate on Harlem, partly because "everyone told me not to work there, so that was where I wanted to work," and partly because Harlem has a higher concentration of heroin pushers than anywhere else in the world. She knew that if she could win acceptance on Harlem's junk sets, she would be able to make buys almost at will.

And win it she did. One junkie spent two hours begging her to give up heroin. She had bought from him a couple of weeks earlier, he had been arrested, and now he was back on the street on bail. Still unaware that Pat was an undercover, he spilled out to her all his problems—the arrest, the bail, the approaching court hearing. "We were walking around the set, him talking to me, and it started going through my mind, 'Maybe he knows who I am, that I'm the one who sent him to jail.' Be-

71

cause he keeps saying, 'Let's go over here, let's go over there,' like maybe he's trying to take me some place. But he wasn't. He was just honestly trying to get me off stuff. He wanted to come home and meet my mother. I was too nice a girl, he said. I was ruining my life. He says, 'You could be so happy. I could help you. I'll make you strong.'

"And then he said, 'But we have to live together, otherwise I won't be able to watch you all the time.' And he went on and on. 'It's no good, it'll only destroy your life. What are you? Fifteen? Sixteen? You look twenty. See how it's aging you? Look at yourself in the mirror. In ten years you'll look forty, if you stay on the stuff. You gotta get off of it. I know it's hard. I know.'

"He was the only person who ever really didn't want me to be on the stuff. Poor soul."

It is a hazard of undercover work that as you cultivate the closeness of your prey, you may also gain affection for him. This "poor soul" syndrome is an emotional luxury rarely indulged in by Patricia, and strictly discouraged by her police associates. "You get so close with them, with the junkies, when you're in undercover that you really know them, and you're accepted by them. And you get to the point where it's not quite so horrifying as it is to someone who's completely disassociated from it. It's more or less like being able to accept it after a while, like it's a part of everyday living almost. And you talk to these people and you almost feel the way they feel, and with them it's just—this is their life. The people that are selling, they're not looked upon as harmful. They're looked at as something great, like he's got something good. He's almost a god image. They never think of this guy as someone who's evil or who's doing harm to them by selling them junk.

"Some of them, you're really friends with them after a while, and you really hate to see them go. But you really don't feel it because they're just all of a sudden removed from the set. You don't take them yourself and have to talk to them later and have to know that right now they're in jail. They're just all of a sudden removed. And actually you're so wrapped up with wanting to get them that once they make the sales to you they just become—he did this and he has to be removed. But some people you get to know so well that you don't like to think about it, that it's as if you have really deceived them. You know, I've had guys where I've arrested them once, I've made buys from them and they've been arrested the first time, and then they'd be out on bail and they'd be selling again and you'd run into them on the street and I'd say, 'What's happening?' And they'd say, 'Well, I'm doing it, but I was busted and I'm on bail and I've got to be careful, so I'm only dealing to a couple of friends, people I really know I can trust. How much do you want?' And you feel, you know, really like Joe Glom.

"When we had to take some guy who was really nice and I'd say to the fellas [other detectives], 'Gee, you know, this guy is really—I hate to see him go,' the fellas would say, 'Hey, Patty! Are you crazy? These people think you're a kid. They have no thoughts at all about selling to you. Why should you feel upset about it? They'd see you in the grave as long as a dollar was coming out of it.' And they would, they really would. They're not nice people."

Occasionally Pat works with informants, and then the totality of her acceptance is particularly critical. When a pusher or user is arrested he is generally given the opportunity to introduce an undercover agent to his connections, with the understanding that this cooperation will be considered at sentencing time. Double-crossing connections takes considerable courage on the junkie's part, and if he is not certain of the undercover agent's ability to play the junkie role, trouble can develop. "If he's not absolutely convinced that you can bring it off," Pat says, "then he just shrivels up inside and he shows it to everyone." Pat has devised an effective means of demonstrating her ability to informants. "Before the informant knows who I am, I just start rapping with somebody else on the street and then walk with him over to the informant and get the two of them to cop with me. And then after we cop I try and make it so I split with the informant, and then after we split I just say to him, 'Oh, by the way, I'm the undercover.' And it knocks them over. And immediately the guy says, 'Like crazy, wow!' And then he has no bad feelings about taking me on a set, because he figures if *he* didn't make me, no one in the world could make me."

When Pat started in undercover, other detectives warned her to listen to her instincts. "If you ever get a feeling about something," they told her, "just take off, go, get out. You can always make another buy, so just get out."

Pat didn't listen. "Things are *always* getting a little eerie. Up there there's whole rows of abandoned buildings, and you have to step over missing stairs to go up to cop off some character in some pitch-black room. So you do sometimes get an eerie sensation, even when there's nothing wrong."

This time, something is wrong. Pat is on the corner of Park Avenue and 123rd Street, talking to three junkies, trying to get them to help her find a connection. As two of the junkies wander off, Pat looks up the block and spots two blacks and a Puerto Rican approaching. The Puerto Rican, whom she has seen before, walks up to her and says, "You looking for something?"

"Yeah," Pat says. "You got something nice?"

Pat tells the man she wants to buy two treys, $3 bags of heroin. He says he has treys, but wants $3.50 for them. "Man," Pat says, "I can get a two-dollar bag around the corner, and all I got is six dollars anyway, so I ain't gonna pay you no $3.50."

"Yeah," the pusher argues, "but these are real knockout bags."

The pusher finally agrees to settle for three dollars a bag. Pat and the junkie standing with her follow the three men down the block. She puts one hand into her coat pocket where she has the six dollars and her automatic. Under the coat she has another gun, a .32 revolver, on a belt. The two blacks turn into a hallway. Pat and her companion go in after them, followed by the Puerto Rican. When Pat is in the hall, the man behind her locks an arm around her neck and presses a knife to her throat. He demands her money. Pat slips her .32 around her waist to the back, where she hopes it will be less easily discovered, then puts her hand in her pocket and grips the automatic.

"Take the bread," Pat chokes, and hands over the six dollars. "That all you have?"

"Man, that's all. You're takin' my copping money. That's all I have."

He throws her aside, and crosses the hallway to help his friends search the other victim. He is finishing that job when a woman comes down the stairs, and Pat and her companion quickly fall in beside the woman and walk with her into the street.

"My first thought," Pat said later, "was, 'Oh, my God, if he starts to search me, I'm gonna have to shoot him.'"

Pat Butler steadfastly refuses to concede that anything she does is dangerous. She stares right through the opaque solidity of undeniable fact, and blasts it into fantasy with one shot of little-girl, Alice-in-Wonderland anti-logic: "A situation's not really dangerous unless you don't get out of it, right? I mean, I just never consider any of it as dangerous. It just doesn't come into my head that way. Like you think about a situation later and maybe you say, 'Oh, boy, that was a little sticky,' but then it's gone. It's over. You got out of it. You're all right. I guess if— well, for instance, if I had had an experience like this other undercover I know, where he had to kill two guys and almost got killed himself, I guess then I would think it was dangerous. But unless you go through it you don't feel it. You don't have the fear. People in undercover who've been beaten up—like one of the guys was beaten so badly they had to completely rebuild his nose. Another fella, they found out he was a cop and he had a gun on them and a guy took a two-by-four and swung it and smashed both his wrists. And after, when they went back on the street, they weren't the same. They lost their heart. That's an expression on the street. You lose your heart. You're afraid then, because you know what can happen. If it happens to you once—really happens—then you're afraid."

Perhaps Pat's make-believe view of the risk around her protects her peace of mind. Certainly it menaces her physical well-being. Stubborn faith in one's invulnerability is a dangerous philosophy on a junk set. While escaping the attacks of muggers, the undercover agent must also avoid an even greater threat. The ultimate disaster is discovery—in undercover language, "a burn." When junkies and pushers on a particular set learn or suspect an agent's identity, he has "taken a burn." Burns come in varying degrees: mild when the suspicion is slight and ill-founded; menacingly intense when there is no suspicion at all, but certain knowledge. At its mildest, a burn can destroy the agent's effectiveness on the set. At its worst, it can destroy the agent. From her own experience, and from the unfortunate adventures of burned colleagues, Pat has developed a number of techniques for remaining cool. When she enters a set for the first time, she speaks to no one. She stands around looking sick and filthy, and waits for someone to approach her. The first couple of pushers who sell to her are left on the set as long as she continues to work it—sometimes weeks or months. If the great number of pushers who sell to Pat and are then picked up creates suspicion, the first two pushers are still around to say, "Hey, man, she cops from me, and I'm out here. What are you talkin' about?"

Pat always tries to cop with a group, reducing the chance that the pusher will remember her. If possible, she convinces the junkies with her to let her carry the money and the junk. They are pleased to have her undertake the most dangerous part of the mission, and she is pleased to have the sales made to her. To avoid circumstances that might place her in the pusher's memory, she tries not to buy when the pusher is down to his last couple of bags, or if he has not been dealing heavily. When the pusher is arrested and arraigned, he learns from the indictment the name of the undercover agent, and the dates of his sales.

"He's sitting in jail," Pat explains, "and he's thinking about that indictment. The undercover's name means nothing to him —no undercover would ever use his real name on the street. In fact, I've had pushers come up to me and say, 'Hey, man, there's some big colored broad out here named Patty Butler. Be careful, man, 'cause she's a cop.' So the name means nothing. Like this article you're writing. They're gonna read that, right? Some of them are, at least the ones in jail. And they might *think* they know who Patty Butler is, but they don't. Even the physical description. Do you know how many white junkie girls there are on the street who have the same description I do? Hundreds. But anyway, getting back to this dealer who's in jail thinking about the indictment. The name might not mean anything, but the dates do, the dates he made the sales. He goes to work on those dates. He thinks about one of those days, trying to remember it, and he says to himself, 'What was I doing that day? Who did I sell to that day? I remember that day now, that was a Tuesday, I wasn't dealing heavy that day. I was broke that day. Wait a minute! I had a couple of extra bags. I sold them to that broad.' Now you're burnt. He's talking to everyone in jail—'Hey, there's this broad out there who's an undercover'—and you're dead. You can forget about it. You have to know the job, and if you don't know the job you can get burnt to death."

When an undercover agent has been burned, he finds out fast. "You get a feeling," Pat says. "You walk on the set and look at one guy and you know immediately you took a burn. If they have suspicions but they're not sure, then the best thing is to stay and push yourself and convince them they're wrong. Eventually they're going to forget their suspicions. But if it's something really concrete, if they've really got you, then you get out."

Pat swears that she is never frightened when a pusher accuses her of working for the cops. "You're too busy thinking of ways to get out of it. If somebody just grabs you and says, 'Hey, I wanna talk to you,' and brings you down into a dark cellar—well, you try to avoid getting into the cellar first of all. You say, 'Hey, man, what are you doin'? I don't wanna go down in no cellar with you.' But you've got to be cool, because many times you buy in cellars and you can't always refuse. You have to go. You don't *really* know what the guy wants. So you go."

Pat is on a junk corner in the Bronx when a man she has never seen before walks up to her on the street. "You lookin' for somethin'?"

"Yeah," Pat says, "I'm lookin' for bams." Bams are glass ampules of an amphetamine junkies like to mix with heroin.

"I got somethin' really nice," the man says. Suspicious, Pat decides to test him. "Well," she says, "I only got two dollars." The going price for a bam is three dollars.

"That's okay, baby, two's fine." Now Pat knows something is wrong. She guesses the man is trying to rob her. But since she's already committed herself to the sale, anything short of eagerness now will create suspicion. She has two dollars in her pocket and more bills in her bra with the automatic. If he robs her and is dissatisfied with the two dollars, she'll be able to reach into her bra for the other bills, and come out with the gun.

The man walks into an abandoned tenement, and Pat follows. They stumble down a dark flight of broken stairs to the cellar. Then he turns abruptly in the darkness and challenges her. "I heard you were the man. You're a cop."

Pat tries to look defiant. "Hey, where'd you get that from? They know me around here. You can ask anybody. But I never saw you before. Who the hell are you?"

He takes a step toward her. "Lemme see your tracks."

Pat stands firm. "Who the hell are you? Whaddya mean, lemme see your tracks? I'm a pros, man, I shoot up in my thighs, and I'm not pulling my pants down for you. And I don't know who you are. Lemme see *your* tracks. Maybe *you're* the man. You came on strong to me that you had somethin' nice, so what's all this? Forget it."

She turns quickly and runs back up the stairs to the street. "I got out of it," she says later, "but now I know the heat's there."

She smiles. "We took like thirty people off that corner, so no wonder."

Like a nightclub comic who anticipates hecklers, Pat has a store of ready-made escapes from predictable crises. She has developed a repertoire of excuses for people who want her to shoot up with them. Sometimes the excuses don't work. She is in a Bronx apartment where she has just bought a five-dollar bag of heroin from a pusher who now commences to explain his house rules. No one leaves with his junk. You buy there, you shoot up there.

Five junkies also have made buys, and are ready to shoot up. Pat explains that she has to divide the bag with her boyfriend who is home sick and will be angry if she gets off without him. The pusher is not even listening. She says she does not have a set of works (the needle and eye-dropper used to inject the drug). A junkie says he will lend her his. She tries a few more previously reliable dodges. The pusher is unimpressed. Suddenly, Pat finds herself with her sleeve rolled up. A junkie hands her his belt. She wraps it around her bicep.

"Okay," she says, and with the belt around her arm she strikes a match and holds it under the cooker. The other junkies, anxious to get off, start shooting up. Pat stalls along, draws the fluid into the eye-dropper, flexes her arm. She glances around the room. The pusher and buyers are either shooting up or starting to nod. She turns aside slightly, shoots the fluid onto the floor and presses the needle against her flesh. She drops the eye-dropper into a glass of water and unfastens the belt. The ruse works.

What does Pat Butler think would happen if it came right down to a heavy burn, alone in an apartment with a pusher who had her gun and shield, and there were no more arguments to be made?

"You can't know. I guess if they felt they could eliminate you without danger to themselves—like, I've spoken to guys where they felt that they wouldn't do anything to a cop, because they figure if you kill a cop, you're dead. Then there's others that would think nothing of it. I've had guys say, 'I heard you were the man, and if I really believed you were the man, you'd be dead now.' And I'd say, 'Are you crazy or something? Where'd you ever get anything like that from?' I'm sure more than half of the pushers would feel that if they could get out of a situation by eliminating you and nobody knowing about it, they would do it. Let's face it, if a guy's facing fifteen years, and if he thinks there's no possible chance that anybody saw me go up there, and he can get away from doing the fifteen years, I think he's going to try."

Pat likes to take drives in the country, and on one rare day off she jumps in a car with a friend and heads for a lake in Connecticut. She spins the wheel, steps on the gas, and zooms the car through heavy crosstown traffic and onto a parkway. She once had a St. Christopher statue on the dashboard, but it's gone now, she can't remember where. (A fellow detective says it leaped from the car in fright somewhere along the East River Drive.)

Her companion asks if male detectives ever resent her. "You know who resents you?" she asks, talking fast, very excited, with no spaces between the words. "The gloms. The do-nothings. No matter how active you are, they'll say, 'Oh, she got in on a hook,' explaining away their own incompetence. They don't want to admit that because they're do-nothings, that's why they're where they are—and because you aren't, that's why you're where you are. Sometimes the fellas in the office have to defend me. Because people are very strange. They always like to look for a snide, cynical, horrid reason for how you got your shield. When I got my shield, it was the greatest

79

experience—you can't imagine what it was like. I felt like I was born."

Pat turns off the parkway and steers the car along country roads, past fields and over streams.

"Did anyone ever accuse you of getting your shield through sex?"

"Oh, I've had that. People have said it. If I wasn't a worker, that would be the reason everyone would give. They would say, 'Oh, well, she's an attractive girl, you know how *she* got the shield.'"

What about a good collar, someone very big, would she use sex for that?

She smiles. "*That* I'd have to think about. Isn't this a lovely road?"

She has arrived at the lake. It is surrounded by grass, and beyond the grass, heavy woods. She stops the car and sits talking some more about the pushers, the fights, the junkies. The words do not match the girl. Inside her little black handbag crouches a detective's shield and a loaded .25 automatic, the gift of a boyfriend. Her companion asks how her dates feel about being out with a cop.

"If I date a fellow who's not in the job," she says, "I don't talk about my job. I don't make my job an exciting, interesting thing because that would put him down. As a woman, the first thing in your mind is to make your date feel important. So you talk about him, not about yourself. If I'm dating a lawyer, for example—well, he has an interesting job. I say I'm in the Narcotics Bureau and I don't discuss it. He probably thinks I'm a secretary or something."

She leans back in the seat and softly insists that "Most dates think of me more as a woman than a detective. I never have a problem with someone feeling strange about kissing me. If I kissed you, I doubt very much if you would think about my being a cop." She smiles. She is very beautiful and very nice. But it is not quite possible to forget about the shield and the loaded automatic.

HANSON

Two days after Det. Butler's death, Lt. Phillip Hanson, Butler's supervisor, was interviewed by this office. He came voluntarily, saying that he felt in some degree responsible for what had happened. He said he wanted to make sure that "certain conversations and information" relating to the case were brought to the attention of the Commissioner. A brief note on Hanson's background: He entered the Academy after graduating from Fordham; served in the 19th Pct. as a patrolman; promoted to sergeant and transferred to the 67th Pct.; then promoted to lieutenant and transferred to present assignment as Group Five supervisor in the Narcotics Bureau. He is forty-five years old. A transcription of his tape-recorded interview follows.

PRESENT: Capt. Henry Strichter,
Internal Affairs Division

Lt. Phillip Hanson

[HANSON 1]

Q: All right, then. From the beginning?

A: Well, Butler had been in the Narcotics Bureau for about a year and a half, undercover all of that time except the first couple of weeks, and always in my group. She was very good—very, very good. She was making more buys than any of the male undercovers. And then one morning in the beginning of June, I think it was a Wednesday, about the second, maybe the third—

Q: We don't need the date, Lieutenant.

A: Yes. Well, she came to my office that morning and asked if she could see me, and I told her to come in and sit down. She asked if she could close the door, and I said yes. I asked her what the problem was. She said there wasn't any problem. She said she thought she was getting into something valuable and had a plan she wanted to discuss with me. She said she had been introduced to a young black dealer called the Stick, about twenty, twenty-one, who was very big in Harlem and had just moved into a flat in Times Square. She said he appeared to be developing new connections and broadening his operations. She said he was very ambitious, buying from big people, and trying to move up to bigger things. She said, too, that he was involved, she wasn't sure to what extent, with black militant politics, Black Panthers, that sort of thing.

I asked her what she had in mind, specifically. She told me that she hadn't made buys from the Stick, that she'd told him she was just chipping. He took a liking to her, cautioned her against using junk, and when she saw him after that she made it a point to look cleaner and to tell him that she was taking his advice.

Q: And then?

A: Then she said he wanted her to move in with him, be his old lady.

Q: Go ahead.

A: I said to her, "You mean live with him?" She said, "That's right. What do you think?"

I said, "Well, what do *you* think?" I mean, she'd been around and she was a big girl and certainly she wasn't any virgin —but shacking up with a black pusher, that was stretching things out a bit. If she'd been one of the black undercover girls, I might not have thought so much about it. But Butler. That was a little . . . So I asked her what *she* thought about the idea. And she was very serious and businesslike. I had thought maybe she wasn't really all that serious about it. But she was. She said, "I thought about it for a long time before I came in here, and the one thing I can't get out of my mind is what it could accomplish if I were with him." She said, "It would be like a window on everything he's doing, and the people around him. There would be a *lot* of information. And not just junk."

She said, "He knows everybody in Harlem, and a lot of people outside, too. He has connections I know about in Times Square and Queens, and I'm sure other places. If I were close to him for a while, it could be very valuable, and I'd be in a position to introduce other undercovers. I could put people in all over."

I asked her how she felt about him.

"He's a dealer." That was her only answer. That's all she said. I asked her if she had thought about the danger. She said she didn't think there would be any danger, that he would never find out who she was. I told her she couldn't be sure of that. She just shrugged, like she wasn't even considering it. Then I asked her if she was absolutely sure she wanted to do it. She said she was if the bureau wanted her to do it, if the bureau agreed about the value of it. I said I would talk to Captain D'Angelo about it and get back to her. And she left.

Q: Who's D'Angelo?

A: My boss, head of all the undercovers, of all three groups.

Q: And you talked to him?

A: Right. That afternoon.

Q: Tell me about that.

A: Well, first you have to understand D'Angelo a little. He's —well, he's got a reputation.

Q: What's that?

A: A hot-shot, fair-haired boy—at least that's what some people thought for a while. He looked good on paper, until you had to work with him.

Q: What do you mean? Where'd you hear that?

A: Before he came in the Narcotics Bureau, we heard about him. You hear you're getting a new boss, you ask around. He got the gold shield with his gun, shot a stick-up man, the guy held up a store on D'Angelo's post and came running out and D'Angelo shot him. It turned out the guy was wanted for other stick-ups and a couple of homicides, and D'Angelo was a hero. They promoted him into the detective division. He was in the 17th squad and he murdered the sergeant's test—one of the highest grades they've ever had, I hear—so he made sergeant over a lot of other guys senior to him, and then a couple of years later, the same thing with lieutenant. But they didn't give him a squad, they made him an aviator, jumping around. A friend of mine who worked with him then said he thought he was God's gift to the department, not to mention the rest of the world. They had to pull him out of bars, off of other guys' broads, and they'd have to drag him out of places and cover for him. And evidently he was supposed to get a squad, and then it got out about his private life—his not-so-private life, I should say—and they just left him there, bouncing around, filling in here and there for this guy and that guy. And after a while it started looking like they might leave him there forever. And then he blitzed the captain's test and they sent him to the Narcotics Bureau, and there were rumors that he was more or less out to pasture, that he'd retire in the Narcotics Bureau.

Q: Any problems with him since he came to Narcotics?

A: No. I mean, not like drinking or women—not that I know of. But truthfully, we never got along too well. He let you know he didn't like where he was and he didn't intend to be around any longer than it would take him to maneuver his way out. I think he figured they'd screwed him and tossed him away to rot in Narcotics. He always gave me the impression he had too many angles running around in his head, thinking things over too much. He was too slick.

Q: You talked to him about Butler's idea?

A: Yes. I saw him in his office and I told him what Butler had said, that she wanted to move in with a black dealer, and what did he think. He almost went into shock. Just the idea, the suggestion, knocked him. He was brushing his hair—he's a very vain guy and he has these silver hairbrushes, and a crew cut, gray hair, and when I came in he was going over the sides of his head with these hairbrushes, one in each hand. And he was just brushing away, very carefully, as if he wasn't interested at all in whatever it was I had to talk to him about. And then when I told him about Butler he put the brushes down on the desk and he said, "Say that again." So I told him again. He said, "You mean she wants to *live* with him? Shack up with him? Sleep with him?"

Q: Is something funny?

A: I'm sorry. I just had to smile thinking about the expression on his face. He was stunned. Because on more than one occasion he'd made a move on Butler himself and she'd just ignored him, like she didn't even understand what he was up to, really put him down. And now after the great Captain D'Angelo has struck out, he's hearing she's planning to shack up with a nigger dealer.

I told him I didn't know if she *wanted* to shack up with the guy or not, but that she certainly said she was willing. *Then* you could see it start to get in there, to go to work on him. After that initial shot to his vanity, he was beginning to see the possibilities. He knew how dangerous it was, but he couldn't resist it. I told him what Butler said about the Stick, and he couldn't resist it. He said, "That's really giving your all for the job, wouldn't you say?"

I said it sure seemed that way to me.

Then he said, "Are you sure that's all she's got on her mind?"

I said, "What do you mean by that?"

He said, "Maybe there's more to it?"

I saw what he was thinking, and I said, "Not a chance. I know Butler. She's been in my group since she came here. Forget that. Not a chance." To D'Angelo, everything was suspicious, nothing was face value. He said, "She's been undercover for over a year, been on the street over a year. Maybe she likes him."

I got a little pissed then, and I said, "Impossible. Forget it."

He said okay, that I knew her a lot better than he did, that he just wanted to be sure. Then he said that before he made up his mind about the idea he wanted to talk to Butler and he wanted to know definitely and precisely what could be expected from the Stick. He told me to call CIB and get a background on the Stick and then after he'd read it we'd talk to Butler again.

Q: And you did that?

A: Yes, sir, I did.

HENDERSON
BACKGROUND

Following are extracts, significant to this case, from CIB's background on Thomas Henderson, a/k/a the Stick.

1. Born 6-23-50 at 359 East 123rd St., Manhattan. First came to attention of NYPD on 3-9-58 as a delinquent (robbery with a knife, paroled to mother). Then 7-22-61 (GL auto., dismissed); 3-8-64 (possession of heroin with intent to sell, NYS Training School, nine months); 11-12-67 (one sale of heroin, reduced to possession, six months, suspended).

2. Henderson has never used narcotics. In his early teens he had a reputation for toughness and viciousness and demonstrated this by taking off narcotics dealers around Harlem. He was in a number of knife fights, but was never permanently marked. Possibly as a result of taking off connections, he started dealing himself, taking over small operations from relatively weak dealers, then building them together until he was known as a primary supplier around 115th, 116th, and 117th Streets (see NB 19-355/69). He has a great capability for violence and a reputation for extreme cleverness.

3. On Feb. 18, 1969, at approximately 3 a.m., an explosion and fire wrecked Henderson's apartment at 239 East 111th Street. Two teenage girls living in the apartment with him were killed. Henderson was out at the time. First reports gave the cause as an explosion in a gas stove. The chief on the scene later noticed what he reported as "curved metal fragments" and marked the fire suspicious. The Fire Marshal's office investigated and found the fire had been caused by two time-fused pipe bombs detonated in the kitchen. The pipes were filled with explosive packed around flashbulbs wired to a clock and battery. The pipes were wrapped in gasoline-soaked towels. Henderson said he had no idea who

88

would want to bomb his apartment. CIB initiated a file. A CIB detective discovered a NB undercover with an informant who had worked for Henderson. The undercover interviewed the informant and made the following report:

"Informant states that 'The Stick has been dealing since he was nine.' He states that by the time Henderson was eighteen or nineteen he was 'the biggest dealer on 115th Street.' He states that because of his good looks and style he always had a lot of good-looking girls with him. The informant further states that Henderson got in trouble with the Black Muslims, or black nationalists, in the neighborhood, who didn't like his style and the girls and especially didn't like him selling junk. They leaned on him heavily to stop dealing, but he wouldn't stop. The informant believes that the explosion was the work of black nationalists who wanted to punish him for refusing to stop pushing."

4. Forwarded from Narcotics Bureau, 2-9-71, Lt. R. Hessen. Undercover reports as follows:

"One last thing. CIB might be interested in something about a guy named Tommy Henderson, a/k/a the Stick. I was at Lexington and 117th Street, talking with two known dealers. One of them, an old guy about fifty-five, seemed interested in impressing the other guy, a teenager. He said, 'They ain't like the Muslims. They ain't gonna try to blow him up. They've made themselves a partner.' He was talking about Henderson. The 'they' he was referring to was the Black Panthers. Maybe it's worth something."

5. Forwarded from Bureau of Special Services, 5-2-71:

Henderson now virtually in the employ of the Panthers. After the explosion in his apartment in 1969, he stopped dealing for several weeks. Then he went back. A few months later a Panther representative (unknown) approached him and told him that they wanted him to stop selling drugs. He kept on dealing. Later another representative told him that if he was going to continue dealing he would be "fined" $500 a week. He paid the fine. His take from drug operations was then in excess of $5,000 a week. The fines were increased steadily. He continued to pay. At the present time, it is believed that he is paying at least 80% of his take to the Panthers. He remarked to an undercover: "The Panthers are worse than the shylocks. They won't let you alone. They keep bleeding you, and the more you give them, the more they want." He told an informant that the Panthers have offered him a role in the organization. He said, "I might as well take it, because sooner or later they'll be taking everything I make anyway." Henderson did not say what "the role" would be. The informant at the time did not want to press.

CURRENT: While maintaining his Harlem operations, and perhaps at the encouragement or insistence of the Panthers, Henderson is extending his operations to the Times Square area. This must be expected to include prostitution, loan-sharking, and gambling, as well as narcotics. In view of his close association with the Panthers, attention must be given to the strong possibility of his becoming criminally involved in militant political activities.

Bureau of Special Services now maintaining Henderson on TEN STATUS. It is requested that his CIB file be redesignated ACTIVE to RED.

[HANSON 2]

The Stick background made Butler's idea look very good. Butler was right about him. D'Angelo called Butler and me into his office and he asked her if she understood what she was proposing, and she said she did. And he said, "You want to live with him?" And she said, "Yes."

D'Angelo said, "You could get killed, you know."

She said, "I don't think so."

D'Angelo just nodded at that. She had been in and out of some very touchy spots, on the street. Then D'Angelo said, "Okay, let me think about it."

And we left.

Q: Then what happened?

A: The next day, the next morning, D'Angelo called me into his office, and he was putting on his jacket and he said, "Let's get out of here. Let's take a walk." And we went up the block to an Italian restaurant and we sat in a booth and ordered drinks. He said, "What do you think?"

I said, "It's dangerous. Very dangerous. She's pretty, she's young, she's white. And the Stick—we know what he is."

He asked me if I thought she could bring it off. I told him I had a lot of confidence in her, that she was the best undercover I'd ever had, male or female, that she'd worked everything, from schools to Harlem to Mafia, never a problem moving with anyone—kids, gangsters, junkies, you name it. If she thought she could manage it, she probably could. I said that in view of what might be gained from the project, it ought to get a lot of serious consideration. He gave me a look when I said that. I guess he thought anything that took his time was serious.

Q: Did you actually recommend that the project be undertaken?

A: Not directly.

Q: Did D'Angelo?

A: Not then.

Q: When did he?

A: Well, I can't say that he ever did, really. Neither of us did. We were just talking about it, discussing how it could be done, and it was just assumed, I guess, that we would go forward with it. It didn't seem possible *not* to do it. The possibilities were so enormous, and Butler was so confident.

Q: No second thoughts?

A: Oh, yes, sir! *Lots* of second thoughts. I was scared as hell about it, and D'Angelo was, too. It was a damned dangerous gamble. D'Angelo pulled a copy of the Stick background out of his pocket, like he'd been carrying it around with him ever since he got it, and he looked it over again there in the restaurant. "Bad man," he said. And he said, "Do you think we should let her do it?"

I said, "We?"

"Who else?"

"You're not going to ask Perna?"

"Ask Perna?" he said. "He'd love the idea, but he'd never be able to approve it. An assistant chief inspector? He'd have to say no. And he'd think we were jerks for asking. Learn something, Hanson. Don't do what the boss says he wants, do what he wants. If you're thinking about consulting Perna, you're thinking about forgetting the whole thing."

He gave me a look then, like asking if that was what I wanted, to forget the whole thing. I guess that's when I could have said no. But I didn't. I didn't say anything. I was greedy, too. Let's face it. I wanted it as much as he did. I have a family, too. We both knew that if it worked, if Butler got good stuff and some big collars developed, we'd come out on top. He wanted a district and I wanted a squad, and this was the way to get it. Simple as that. A squad and then—this kind of thing stays with you. It keeps pushing you right along. I didn't want to spend the rest of my life supervising undercovers. And I was influenced by Butler's confidence. She was *so* sure she could do it. She didn't think she'd get killed, and I didn't either.

So we talked it over. We decided that the important thing was that nobody know about the shacking-up part except us and

Butler. I said I'd talk to her and tell her not to mention it to anyone else. Not that she'd be inclined to, anyway.

Q: Was she ever present when you were discussing this with D'Angelo?

A: Never. She wasn't involved in the planning.

Q: What about the planning?

A: We were talking it over in the restaurant, and D'Angelo said, "If something goes wrong, there won't be any covering it up. The PC and everyone else in town is going to break balls till they know how and why." And then he said—and this shows you how his mind worked—he said, "But the critical thing won't be that she got killed. That could be handled. Cops get killed all the time. It'll be that she got laid. And that she had *permission* to get *laid*. That the New York City Police Department, *officially*, gave her permission to go out on a job and get fucked. That'll be the killer. Can you hear the PC? 'You mean you knew that young, innocent, pure, pretty little girl was intending to shack up with one of the heaviest black heroin dealers in the city, and you let her?' There's no answer to that question."

"Let's hope it will never be asked."

"Hope, hell. We need insurance that it *can't* be asked. We've got to forget that she said anything about shacking up. All she suggested was that she get close to him, get to know him, hang around with him. She never said anything about shacking up. And then, on top of that, we need something to make it clear that we were aware of the dangers of her spending that much time with him, letting him get that tight with her—that we took every possible precaution, even extraordinary precautions."

I asked him if by that he meant an extra team. Because half the time the team she's working with can't keep up with her. If two guys can't give her coverage when she goes into a hallway to cop, how the hell will a double team help? He said he was thinking of maybe undercovers. I said I didn't think that'd be any better. The more people you have, the more chance they'll stumble over each other. I said, "If one of the undercovers got burned, it'd throw suspicion on everyone around him." I said I thought she'd be safer working alone, and I was sure she'd rather work alone.

D'Angelo said, "Is that what we'll tell the PC? 'We didn't give her protection because she prefers to work alone'?"

Then he got up and paid for the drinks and on the way back to the house he said, "Think about it. Come up with something. I'll see you tomorrow."

And I spent all night going over ideas. She didn't need our protection. Or at least not any protection I could think of that would do her any good. I was afraid that D'Angelo, by trying to put up a show of giving help, would set up something that'd make it tougher for her than it already was. The only thing I could think of that might do any good at all would be something to reinforce the Stick's idea that she's okay. So if he heard anything about her not being right, he'd be more likely to disregard it.

The next day D'Angelo called me out of my office and we went back to the restaurant. I think he was getting a little paranoid. A bug in his office?

He said he'd been thinking about the problem, and one thing he wanted to do was put Butler in a SAC. He said, "It's not because of what I said, that maybe there's more than she's telling us. I believe you on that. Like I said, you know her a lot better than I do. But you can't be too careful, and having that kind of contact might be a good thing. Anyway, there's nothing to lose, so we'll SAC her."

Then I told him my idea, and he went for it. "It's an old trick," he said, "but it might work. Anyway, it gives us something. Who does the Stick think she is now?"

I said, "A runaway."

He said, "So if the Stick heard that someone had been asking around for her, a cop—"

"It would strengthen his belief that she is what she says she is—or maybe a little more. That she's not just a runaway. That she's wanted."

"Or, anyway, that she sure as hell isn't a cop."

So we worked it out. We wanted a detective just to go through the motions, make it look good, but not find her. Get close, close enough for the Stick to hear about it and be convinced. D'Angelo didn't want to tell the detective that it was a ruse. He didn't want to tell anyone anything. The reason he gave—he said he wanted to be positive that the cop who was supposed to be looking for her didn't mention the job to someone else, like his partner maybe, who would pass it on, and eventually the wrong guy hears it. And there I agreed with him. You don't want something leaked, you don't talk about it. To anyone. It's the only sure way. And D'Angelo said if the cop did run into Butler he didn't want him reacting any way except like a cop who really was looking for her. D'Angelo didn't even want to tell Butler what was up. But I talked him out of that. I said I'd just let her know that if she heard any rumors about her being a fugitive, it was coming from us and not to wonder about it. And I said to D'Angelo, "What if our man does slip up and find her? Maybe he's not as dumb as we think he is."

D'Angelo said, "He won't find her. I'll get some jerk-off and I won't tell him enough to be able to find her in a year. And anyway, we'll tell him if he finds her, not to make a collar. Observe and report."

I said, "Where are we going to find this guy? All the men in the bureau know Butler."

He said, "She's going to be shacked up with him in the 16th, so it'll have to be a man from that squad. Don't worry about it. I'll set it up with the squad commander."

And that was that.

[LOCKLEY 5]

Q: Then Crunch never got you a collar.

A: No, but he didn't have a chance to really, because right after that I started this case. I went on my swing after that, and then I was back on a Tuesday and the Owl called me into his office.

Q: Tell me about that.

A: Well, first I have to explain something about the way I felt. In the squad there, you know, they have this bulletin board covered with wanted flyers and all these missing-person flyers. And of course no one ever looks at them, but when I first came into the squad I looked at them a lot. They're really pathetic. These class yearbook pictures, you know, of kids all very clean-cut looking, and the description, and how they're missing from home, please contact the Darien, Connecticut, police department. And you know they don't look anything like these pictures any more, and that if they came to New York, and to Times Square especially—well, the parents can just pack it in.

And you look at those pictures and you wonder what the kids look like now, and what they're doing now, and you look at the pictures and you try to imagine that this girl is on junk now and a whore and all that.

Well, one day a guy came into the squad and he's about thirty, and he says he's in New York looking for his sister, and what can he do. He says he went to a private detective and the detective told him just to hang around Times Square and he'd probably see her 'cause if you spent enough time in Times Square you saw everyone. He was from Cleveland and he came here he told us on a bus. Schulman asked him what he paid the private detective and he said fifty dollars. So we had the guy

96

fill out the form and we took a picture he had of the kid and we told him we'd keep our eyes open.

I felt terrible after he left. We tacked the picture up on the board with all the others, and that was it. I really felt like I should have done something more for him. But what can you do? He had no idea at all where she was. He didn't even know she was in New York for sure. All the same, I felt like I should have done something.

Well, this is all preamble, so you'll understand a little how I felt after I came in that Tuesday, after the thing with Crunch and the undercover. The Owl called me into his office. It was about 3:30 in the afternoon, I'd just come in for a four-to-twelve, and he said he had something for me, a runaway. He said he was taking me off the chart for a day. He said the runaway was a girl, five-feet-four, 110 pounds, blond hair, called Chiclet, supposed to be in the Times Square area. He was very curt about the whole thing, like it was wasting his time. He said, "I can't tell you anything else because I don't know. All they gave me for a name is Chiclet, which is probably all she's using on the street anyway, and it keeps the real name out of the papers. It's a contract, a politician's kid or something like that, so someone has to make a show, go through the motions. But don't bust your balls over it, just check out a few bars, spread the name around. No one expects you to find her. Go through the motions and file a report and everyone'll be happy. And if you do fall over her, give me a call. Don't pick her up."

Like some guy with influence has leaned on someone downtown to get off their asses and find his daughter, so they've got to do something more than just stick her picture up on the wall. But even then they don't take it seriously. Just some kid, even a big shot's kid—forget it. Go through the motions. You're not gonna find her anyway, so don't break your balls. What he was telling me was just go have a few beers and then write a report and forget it.

Q: What day was this now?

A: This was Tuesday. It was the first day back after my swing. I was working four-to-twelve and the next day I'd do a four-to-twelve again. I left the Owl's office, and I was pretty pissed off. It made me mad for the Owl to come right out and say he was giving me some shit assignment where all I was expected to do was sit around in bars. The whole attitude made me mad. It was typical. Go through the motions. Don't take it seriously. Just cover yourself. The report I write covers the Owl, and he endorses it and sends it on up and eventually whoever the big shot is gets a hand job about how the department turned things upside down looking for his daughter.

So I go out and I start walking up 43rd Street toward Broadway, thinking what to do, how to find this girl. And I really want to find her. I was thinking maybe this doesn't have to be such a horseshit assignment after all. Right? Some poor bastard wants his daughter back while there's still something left of her.

I was thinking, what would Crunch do. Crunch would find that girl in ten minutes. He'd know just where to go, what to do, who to talk to. I thought, what the hell do I know. I don't know anything. I know her name's Chiclet and she's supposed to be in Times Square. So, like the Owl said, I might as well begin with the bars. A name like Chiclet, anyone who heard it ought to remember it.

Then I think that it's lucky now I never got around the precinct too much because the fewer people who know I'm a cop the better, and I'm also lucky because I don't really look that much like a cop, in fact I don't look like a cop at all. So I get on the train and go home and put on some jeans and a polo shirt, like a tennis shirt, and I go in my father's closet and borrow an old ankle holster he has, and I'm ready to go, back to Times Square. Except that I can hardly walk. I keep limping, from the weight of the piece on my ankle. I remember I was wondering how Crunch did it, and trying to compensate some way for the weight so I wouldn't limp. But I couldn't do it. Then I figured, what the hell, people will just think I've got a sore leg.

I start on 45th Street, the really bad places, they're all wrong there, and I go to the discothèque places, into the Bandwagon, and Gypsy's, and they never heard of the girl.

"Who?" They're yelling at me, and no one can hear anything because of the music. And I'm yelling. "Chiclet!"

"Who?"

"Chiclet!"

I'm yelling my lungs out, and the guy shakes his head.

I try bartenders, bouncers, waiters. Nothing. Then I hit—oh, I hit everywhere. Brown's, the fag place, and I ask some queen waiter and he gives my jeans the once-over like he's gonna get in them with me, and he shakes his head.

I go *everywhere*. Toppers, West 47th Street. That was funny. They were watching a fight on TV, and it was a black kid and a white kid fighting. And I'm standing at the bar, trying to look nonchalant, the only white guy in there, and there's this old guy next to me, drunk as hell, but a nice guy, laughing at everything, just having a good old time, and he turns around and he sees me and he's surprised to see me, because I'm white, and he looks at the TV set and he says to me, yells at me, "Man, you got to *cheer!* You got to *cheer!*" I'm the only white guy there, right? And I'm letting my whole race down because I'm not cheering for the white guy.

They never heard of her either. I'm really getting discouraged. I've been in about twenty bars all over the place, and just a lot of blank stares. So I take another walk around the block, just thinking, by now it's about nine, ten o'clock at night, and I say, "Well, I'm on the wrong track." Obviously. She doesn't go to bars. She hasn't got a boyfriend taking her around bars, she's not hanging around in them herself. So the only other thing is drugs. And that means kids, especially around here. So where do the kids go, and I remember this luncheonette on 49th Street that's always filled with kids, and Crunch told me it was where the A&R men went to lay off IDs. He said for fifty bucks you could buy a whole set—driver's license, credit cards, the whole thing. So I think, well, I'll walk by and take a look.

And the place is full of kids, as usual, sitting around in the booths. I go limping in and sit at the counter and order a cup of coffee, and right behind me in one of the booths there's these five kids, two guys and three girls. One of the guys you can tell is really the top guy. He's about nineteen, very tall, thin, good-looking, and he has a very composed, confident air, as if he's been around here for years and years and knows everything and everybody there is to know.

He's wearing a bright orange shirt with this enormous, billowing collar, and a green handkerchief or something around his neck. And a leather vest, and this *hat*. You should have seen this hat—white with a big wide brim turned up on one side the way you see pictures of men wearing hats in Australia—and he has a feather, a big long yellow feather stuck in the band, like Robin Hood or something.

And this guy you can tell really has the girls in this place turned on good. The other guy at the table is a really sick-looking little kid, quiet, pale, pimply, skinny, smiling all the time, never talks, just sits there, happy to be near the other guy, I guess, and smiling.

I remember thinking that almost any one of the girls in this place—maybe fifteen, twenty of them—could be Chiclet. I thought of just standing up and yelling, "Hey, Chiclet! You're wanted on the phone!" But I figured that wouldn't be too cool, would it.

Anyway, so I watch this guy with the hat, and all the girls and a lot of the guys in the place are all over him, coming up to talk to him, and he's being Mr. Charm, and he obviously is the kid I need to talk to.

So I spend about ten minutes trying to think of what to say, should I tell him I'm a cop. And I decide no, it's better not, better just to bluff along. So I get off the stool and I limp over and I say to him, "Excuse me, I'd like to talk to you." Very polite and nice I was.

He says, "Very well." Like that, "Very well."

The girls smile. One of them is very young, maybe fourteen, and pretty, very innocent-looking, lost-looking. She's wearing a blue button-down man's shirt with a red sweater over it, the sweater sleeves cut off above the elbow, and it looks nice. I mean the sleeves are all coming unraveled and it gives her a kind of ragamuffin look, but nice, too, like who cares, I like it so I'll wear it. And she looks at me and then she looks at the other girls and sees they're just staring at the hat guy, kind of smirking, so she starts staring at him, too, only she can't quite make the smirk. She needs a little more practice. Well, it's obvious he's not moving and if I want to talk I've got to do it here.

I say, "I'm looking for a girl. I thought maybe you could help me."

He says, "Maybe." Smiling, very charming.

I say, "Her name's Chiclet, she hangs around here. Maybe you know her."

He looks at the fourteen-year-old, just gives her a look, and she moves out of the booth without a word and walks out of the place.

"Chiclet," he says. "So what about her?"

"Nothing," I say. "Just that I'm looking for her. We used to be friends and I haven't seen her for a while and I heard she was here."

Then he gets up and tells the others he'll be right back and says to me, "Let's see," and walks out to the street with me following.

"I think I can fix you up," he says, and we walk down the street, very slowly, just sort of ambling along.

We turn left on Seventh Avenue, left again on Fiftieth, and we go into this junkie hotel there, the Christopher. The lobby is loaded with old people just sitting around staring like zombies, not seeing anything, and whores and junkies running in and out. So Robin Hood with the hat says something to the old man at the desk and the man gives him a key and up we go in the elevator. Now we get outside the room, and the guy says, "Fifty dollars."

And I say, "You're crazy, what for?"

"For Chiclet."

I say, "She's in there?"

He nods.

"I haven't got fifty dollars," I say.

"I'll take what you've got," he says, very nice, not pushing it, acting, you know, really like he was just trying to do me a favor, just a really nice guy, but thinking that maybe he deserved something for going out of his way like this. I give him twenty dollars and he turns around and goes down in the elevator.

I knock on the door, and this girl's voice says come in. And I go in and of course it's the fourteen-year-old from the luncheonette. She's standing by the window, looking out, trying to be very casual. She probably saw Elizabeth Taylor or someone staring out a window like that in a movie, but it's pretty ridiculous here because what you see out that window is the back of a neon sign and a fire escape with old bottles on it.

I say, "You're not Chiclet."

She turns around and looks at me. "Who's Chiclet?"

"The girl I said I was looking for."

101

"I didn't hear." She's got the sweater off and she starts to unbutton the shirt. "Aren't I as nice as Chiclet?"

"Yeah," I say, "you're fantastic, but you don't understand. I really *am* looking for a girl named Chiclet."

"You don't have to be embarrassed about it." She's lying down on the bed now, still playing around with the buttons, doing some kind of scene.

"I'm not embarrassed about it," I say. "I'm just *really* looking for a girl named Chiclet."

"That's not what Billy thought."

Billy's Robin Hood, the hat kid, right? So I say, "It doesn't matter what Billy thought."

She's trying to be very cool about the whole thing, but she's really nervous as hell. Stupid as hell, too.

"Billy thought you were looking for a girl, just any girl."

"Billy was wrong."

"Aren't I as nice as Chiclet?"

"I don't know. I mean, yes, probably. Maybe nicer. Do you do everything Billy tells you to do?"

"I'd do anything for Billy. He's really groovy."

"Why?"

"He's just a groovy guy. He's the grooviest guy I ever met. We're going to get married. Not now because I'm too young, but when the time's right we will."

"Why's he such a great guy?"

"Because he helps everybody," she says. "Like hundreds and hundreds of people that he helps. I was just walking around, and I hadn't eaten for two days or anything, right out here by the Christopher, this hotel that we're in now, and he came up to me and asked me if I wanted something, and he was so nice, he's got a really groovy smile, don't you think? He bought me a hamburger and we talked and ever since then everything's been great, for about a week already, really groovy. He introduced me to all his friends, really groovy people, people like him who'd do anything for you. He even bought me this outfit, isn't it groovy?"

She gets up so I can see the shirt and miniskirt, and starts rebuttoning the buttons. "And he's got nothing out of it for himself. He's just always doing things for other people and he never asks to get anything back from it. I think that's really the way everyone should live. Don't you?"

"What about the twenty dollars I gave him," I say. "Before I came in, I gave him twenty dollars. He got that back from it."

"He *deserves* that," she says, very indignant.

"For what?"

"For *everything*. He lets me stay in his apartment, and he has a friend who's going to get me a job as a model and then I'll earn a hundred dollars an hour, as a model. Are you going to ask him for the money back?"

"I don't know," I say. I'm out of it at this point, really out of it. I mean I'm just a little country boy from Massapequa. She was pretty, but *dumb*. And let's face it, street wise I'm not. My father could have been a plumber for all the—I mean he never brought his job home, not at all. Once when I was eight I think he'd been on a really ghoulish homicide, a child molester it must have been because he came home and he sat me down and told me all about child molesters and to look out for them. I was telling it around school the next day and the teacher heard and asked me and I told *her* all about child molesters, and she came home with me and talked to my father and I guess she told him she thought eight was too young for that kind of information.

Anyway, back to this fourteen-year-old, this fourteen-year-old runaway whore—looking at her, hearing her, it was so *pathetic*.

So anyway, she asks if I'm going to try to get the money back, and I say I don't know. Then I'm leaving and she says, "Was Chiclet your girlfriend?"

"Yeah," I say. What the hell.

"She ran away from you?"

"Maybe."

"She probably misses you as much as you miss her."

"Yeah, I guess."

"She was around here," she says.

"Sure."

"Honest, she was. I don't know why Billy didn't tell you."

I look at her. How many times can you get conned in one night?

"Honest she was. Don't tell Billy I told you. But if you really love her and she loves you, nothing should keep you apart."

"What did she look like?"

"I don't remember exactly because she was only in and out once, but she was pretty. I remember her because she was with a groovy black guy, and he was talking to Billy for a while and I remember the chick this black kid was with had a funny name. I remember thinking that it was a groovy name for a chick with a black kid, I don't know why, just for some reason."

"What was the black guy's name?"

"Billy called him the Stick. That's a funny name, too, isn't it? He was a really groovy kid."

"What did he look like?"

"Really groovy. Your age. Tall and thin and dressed groovy, like Billy, and nice and polite to everyone, shaking hands with everyone and smiling and everything, and very, just *nice,* like you. Not really like you, you know, because he was black and you're white."

So I thank her. Oh, brother. And I walk over to the door.

"What's wrong with your leg?" she says. "Did you hurt your foot?"

"No. Nothing." And I leave.

Now I'm excited. I'm outside in the hall, and I'm *excited.* Because right then I *know* I'm going to find Chiclet.

I go back to the luncheonette, and too good to be true, there Billy is, still there. And now I have a plan. This guy knows where Chiclet is, and I'm going to find out from him, I don't care how. So I take the piece out of the holster and put it in my pocket.

He's with some different people now, but still in the booth. I go up and I tell him I want to talk to him. And he gives it the big smile and says okay. No "very well" this time. Just okay. And he sits there. And I say, "Privately, if you don't mind."

So he gets up and he comes outside, and I just walk a couple of steps to get away from the windows where his friends are, and then I palm the piece and slap him hard with it on the ribs and I say, "That's a piece, Billy, so let's take a walk."

I'm really coming on like Crunch now, a real hot cop, right?

I walk him back to the hotel and I say to the desk man, "I left something in the room. We'll just be a couple of minutes."

And he gives me the key. We go up. Billy sits on the bed and I sit in a chair. I aim the piece at him and I say, "Where's Chiclet?"

He says, "You a cop?"

"Where's Chiclet?"

"I don't know. What's wrong with Samantha?"

Samantha, right? Well, that figures.

"What's wrong with Samantha is that she's not Chiclet. Stop bullshitting. Where's Chiclet?"

"I'm afraid you've gotten something confused. I don't know any Chiclet."

"Okay," I say. "You don't know any Chiclet." He's still on the bed, looking very relaxed, really, not worried about anything. I guess he's had guns pointed at him before. So very quickly I break the piece and drop out the cartridges and close it again. I put the cartridges in my pocket. They're all out now, but I tell him, "This is a Colt detectives' special .38. It has six chambers. I just emptied five of them."

"Now, look," he says, but still very cool, "I don't know any Chiclet. If I knew her, I'd tell you. Why not? What reason would I have not to tell you? I'd have told you the first time you said her name, wouldn't I? Why would I send Samantha up here like that if I knew you were really looking for some chick named Chiclet?" He smiles.

"Because you've got reasons for not talking about Chiclet, and if some guy comes around asking for her, what's it to you to tell him anything. But on the other hand, while you're at it, why not beat the idiot for a few bucks."

I mean, he probably figured he was safe. I got value for money, right? Why should I beef?

So I've got the piece aimed at him, and I tell him there's one round left in it, which of course there isn't, it's empty as hell, and I point it at his foot, and I say, "I'm gonna ask you where Chiclet is. I'm gonna ask you six times. Every time I'm gonna raise my aim a little. So if you're a gambler, and you don't want to tell me where she is, you can guess whether you lose a foot, a kneecap, your balls, your belly, or your brains. Now—where's Chiclet?"

Well, this doesn't really have the desired effect at all. He leans back on the bed on one elbow and just stares straight into my eyes. Doesn't even look at the piece. Him and that stupid hat.

So I pull the trigger. *"Click."* He just stares.

I aim at his kneecap. "Where's Chiclet?" He stares. I pull the trigger. *"Click."*

I aim at his crotch. "Where's Chiclet?" He stares. I pull the trigger. *"Click."* He's even smiling a little.

Well, I know by now this isn't going to work, and I'm finding it very hard about this time to maintain the proper Mickey Spillane atmosphere in the room. I can tell that the initiative is very quickly flowing over to the other side. So I finish out my threat, and I point the gun at his head, feeling like a real asshole now because it's so obvious I'm full of shit. I mean he knows it and I know it, and here I am with an empty gun at his head, pulling the trigger like some kid playing a little game or something.

So it clicks again and then he stands up, still with this little smile, this smirk, and slowly, like he's just too damned bored by the whole scene, he gets up from the bed and walks to the door, and he's very theatrical about the whole thing. I mean like he's had about five minutes while I've been pulling the trigger to figure out how he's going to make his grand exit, and he gets to the door and he doesn't even turn around, just over his shoulder, and softly like he doesn't give a damn if I hear him or not, he says, "Samantha was too good for you."

And he closes the door and I'm sitting there alone with my piece in my hand, feeling like the biggest jerk-off in the history of the world.

And then I start getting mad. It makes you mad, you know, when you make a real ass of yourself. And remember, this guy, this Robin Hood guy, this Billy with the hat, he *knows* where Chiclet is. And he won't tell me. That makes me mad, too.

So between him not telling me and me making a jerk of myself, I start getting really angry. And then it gets like to the top, and it blows. I shove the cartridges back into the piece and I go out the door and he's standing in the hall waiting for the elevator with his back to me. And I don't know why, I didn't think or anything, I know I didn't know I was going to do it when I went into the hall, but I don't say anything. I just all of a sudden fire a shot into the floor.

106

What a *noise!* Have you ever heard a gun fired in a hotel hallway? It about busted my eardrums.

And Billy just freezes, and his arms shoot up like they're on strings. He doesn't even turn around to see what happened.

So a second ago I was mad as hell, and now I'm still mad but I'm scared, too, mostly scared. Because I can see the desk man downstairs already dialing the cops, and I know a Shots Fired on this block gets priority action. I can see about four sector cars and the sergeant and the combat car pouring into the block in about half a minute.

So I grab Billy, and I tell him to put his arms down, and we go back in the room and out the window and down the fire escape to the courtyard between the buildings there, where they keep the garbage cans, and all the whores and junkies throw their garbage down. And we get down there and I put him up against a wall and I say, "Okay, now tell me where's Chiclet."

And do you know, this obstinate bastard *still* tells me he doesn't know any Chiclet?

So I hit him with the piece. I hit him hard with it right across the mouth. He starts to put his hand up to his mouth and I hit him again. I think I hit him about four times or five maybe, in the face. Once I started I could see it was—I don't know how to explain it, like before that he had really been on top. I mean I was in *his* place with *his* friends, and I didn't know what to do or what the rules were or anything like that, do you understand? And then when I was hitting him and he had his hands up and his knees were buckling and I could feel the metal really *hitting,* I felt like everything had reversed, because he hadn't expected that, he'd made a mistake, so he didn't know so much after all.

Anyway, I finally get control of myself again and I stop hitting him and I get a look at his face there in the dark and it's a bloody mess, and his hands are all bloody and he has blood all over his shirt, and now I hear the sirens, and I know some cop is gonna start flashing a light down here from one of the hotel windows and then I'm gonna have to run for it and there's gonna be more shots fired, so I say, "Tell me, you—" I don't remember what I called him. "Where is Chiclet?"

And this time he gives it up. "She's with a guy called the Stick. A spade. He has a loft on 47th Street."

"Where on Forty-seventh?"

"Seventh. There used to be a dance studio there."

His face is really a mess. But he's very matter-of-fact now. He has his shirt off and he's wiping his face and he's talking very calmly, like now he's telling me what I want to know, and that's that.

So I leave him and I walk down an alley and into the hotel on the other side, on 48th Street, not the hotel we were in, and I go in the men's room in the bar and I lock myself in a stall and I wipe my hands off with toilet paper. And the gun, which is practically dripping with blood, has little pieces of skin pinched under the hammer.

And then I wash my hands, and I go out on Forty-eighth and up to the corner, to Seventh Avenue, and left, and here come a couple of sector cars with the dome lights going, and I walk on down to Forty-seventh.

That corner, Forty-seventh and Seventh, is all light, there's this Orange Julius place there, and a hamburger place, and it's very light, lots of people, and I start looking for this loft, which is difficult because I didn't think when I was pounding Billy to ask which corner of Forty-seventh and Seventh. So I'm standing there looking up at the windows, wondering which look like thcy might havc had a dance studio, and I'm looking around and I see Joey on the corner there—Joey without any legs?—I see Joey there with his pencils, and I say hello to him and he remembers me from the time I helped rescue his board out of the river, and he says, "Hi," very nice, like he's not going to sink his teeth into my leg or anything. So I sit down on a step in the hallway there by the hamburger place and he rolls over and I ask him can he help me, and he says what do I need.

"I'm looking for someone who lives in a loft here, but I can't find it, at Forty-seventh and Seventh."

And he says, "Which corner?"

"That's the problem. I don't know. But it used to be a dance studio."

"What's his name, the man you're looking for?"

"The Stick. That's what they call him. I don't know his real name."

"A colored guy?"

"Yeah."

108

"You're looking at the place now," he says. "It's that, right there."

He points to a row of fourth-floor windows right across the street, just above where we're sitting, above one of those gypsy shops.

He says, "It used to be a dance studio. Only after it was a dance studio, it was a discothèque, with go-go girls who danced in the windows there, and you could see them from the street. I used to sit over there on the corner and watch them dancing in the windows, and all the traffic coming down Seventh Avenue slowed up to watch. It closed a year ago. It was empty until this spade took it a couple of months ago. It must be huge, the place."

"What's he look like?"

"He's good-looking, if you like spades. He's always got two or three girls hanging around him. He's a young guy, twenty, twenty-one, your age. I never saw him till he took that loft and then he's in and out a lot, with these girls like I said and with a lot of people, other spades and some nice-looking people too, mostly kids, so he's gotta have something going up there. But he's in for it now, right? Or you wouldn't be looking for him?"

"It's not really him I'm looking for," I tell him. "I'm looking for a girl who's with him. Her name's Chiclet. You ever hear of her?"

He shakes his head.

"She's supposed to be about five-four, 110, blond hair."

"I don't know. He's with a lot of girls, white and black."

And then he stops talking and he's looking across the street, and I look across the street too, and a group of people up by the corner are getting out of two cabs. And then they all stand around for a while talking and then four of them leave and start down the block across the street from us, heading toward the building with the Stick's loft in it.

"That's him," Joey says.

There's this tall, good-looking black and two other black guys, older and shorter and fatter, and a white girl, blond, very pretty, about seventeen, and I say to Joey, "Hey, I *know* her." Because I had seen her before on the street, right there in the same block on Forty-seventh with Crunch, and I'd told Crunch that she looked like a nice kid, a runaway that hadn't got too deep into things yet. So I wasn't too happy to see her waltzing around with the Stick and his friends. He looked rough. Good-looking, but rough. He had on this long black fur coat and wide floppy kind of hat, something like Billy's, only it was black.

They get to the building and go inside and we see lights go on up in the loft, only you can't see anything because all the windows are painted over, different colors, some red, some blue, some yellow. And I say to Joey, "That's her, Joey. That's gotta be her. You ever see her around here before?"

He shakes his head, still looking up at the windows. "No, I never did."

My heart's pounding now. I'm excited as hell. Because I've found her, right? I fish around in my pocket and I get a dime and I give it to Joey and I take one of his ball-points—a felt-tip, not a ball-point—but neither of us has any paper, so I write the number on the palm of his hand, and I say, "Look, Joey, I'm going to watch to make sure she doesn't come out. You call this number and leave word for Lieutenant Seidensticker that Detective Lockley found Chiclet, and where we are."

Now Joey is excited, too, and he wants to help, but he looks at me apologetically, like he's letting me down, and he shrugs, and he says, "I can't."

And I think, what a creep I am. So I say, "I'm sorry, Joey. It doesn't matter, anyway. It's better this way. You wait here and I'll call." And I stand up.

"What'll I do if she comes out?"

Now that's a good question. "If they walk some place, just try to keep up and I'll look for you, I'll ask around and I'll find you, and if they take a cab get the plate number, or if you can stall them, maybe—"

I don't know what to tell him. I just want to call the Owl. I run across the street to the phone booths there, and of course they're all smashed up because of the junkies. So I go up to Forty-eighth. Same thing. Forty-ninth. Same thing. Then I go into the Taft Hotel, and there's a bank of about ten phones and they're all being used. So I run like hell into the Abbey, and there's an empty booth and it's working and I dial the squad.

EAGEN

After the Lockley interviews were completed, Lt. Lyon of this office found the cripple Joe Eagen at the intersection of 48th Street and Broadway. He talked with him in the back seat of a car while a detective drove. The conversation was recorded. Transcription follows.

PRESENT: Lt. William Lyon,
Internal Affairs Division

Det. Michael Roth,
Internal Affairs Division

Joe Eagen

Q: Hey, Joey!

(Street sounds. Garbled voices. Car door slams.)

There you go. Comfortable?

(Garbled conversation. Car door slams.)

A: . . . for a couple of minutes.

Q: It won't take long. We'll just drive around for a while. It's not anything about you. We thought maybe you could help Detective Lockley.

A: Just so long as it don't take too long. I can't be away more than a couple of minutes. I'm only doing it 'cause I'd like to help Lockley. I read about him in the papers. I was the first one who saw him come out of the apartment, you know. I already talked to Schulman.

Q: We want to talk about some things Schulman might have missed. You read the papers so you know Lockley's in trouble, and we heard you and him were friends so we thought maybe you could help him out a little.

A: What do you want to know?

Q: Everything from the beginning. How'd you meet Lockley?

A: I dunno. Long time ago. On the street. And Bellevue, mostly in Bellevue. I've been in there a lot and last time, just a few days ago, Lockley was there, too. We used to talk.

Q: What'd you talk about?

A: Why don't you ask him?

Q: We did, Joey.

A: Then you know already.

Q: Something he couldn't tell us that maybe you can—

A: Yeah?

112

Q: You spend a lot of time around Duffy Square there, Forty-seventh and Seventh, where the Stick had his flat—

A: Yeah.

Q: Ever see anything?

A: Lots of things. Mostly dogshit.

Q: Ever see anything of the Stick?

A: Yeah. I used to see him around since he moved in two or three months ago. Like I told Lockley, he was always in and out with girls and other spades and kids. I knew he was up to no good in there.

Q: Any suspicions about what exactly he might have been up to?

A: No. I heard drugs, but so what. You could say that about anyone around there. I figured drugs, probably.

Q: Ever see her around there?

A: I saw that picture in the paper. The same picture. No. The first time I saw her was that night I was with Lockley. But I couldn't be completely positive. The Stick came in and out with a lot of girls, and I didn't know I was supposed to be keeping score. Where are we going?

Q: Just riding around. Tell me what happened that night.

A: When I found the Stick and the girl?

Q: Right.

A: I was just there on the corner and Lockley's there and he asks me about some spade he's looking for lives on that corner, that intersection, only he don't know which corner. We're talking about which spade, which corner, and he says it's not really the spade he's after, it's this girl. And then the Stick comes by and I tell him that's the Stick and he says this girl with him is the girl he's after.

He has a phone number and he goes to call it and tells me to watch the door to the building they went in and to follow them if they come out. And just after he leaves they come out and I try to keep up with them. But that's not so easy. Most people don't know how hard something like that is. Especially at that time of night. At that time of night usually I wouldn't even try to move, through all those people, all those dirty fuckin' legs. People don't care, they don't give a shit, even when they see you, if they ever look down, they don't *even* see you. Everything on the street is shit to them, it's all fair game for

113

throwing stuff. I get set on *fire* by cigarettes. They don't have any respect for anyone—drop everything on you, spit on you. You should see these boots after a day. You think I wear them 'cause of the sidewalk? I wear them 'cause of the shit and the filth. You talk about pollution and cars and buses. You don't get it till it's six feet high. I get it right out of the pipe. You worry about cars splashing mud on your *clothes*. I get it in the *mouth*. Some clown opened a cab door and it hit me in the chest and took me right off the board. I get dogs. This broad—

Q: Joey—

A: This broad who walks dogs for people, ten dogs at a time, she runs right over me with her fucking dogs. I'm in a fucking forest of dogs, and I reach out and I grab this collie's balls and I yank, and she's *still* looking for that dog. And she don't come around there with her shitting dogs no more. You ever a mounted cop?

Q: No, Joey. I—

A: I used to work the theaters. I don't even go near over there any more. I was—

Q: Joey, you said you tried to follow the Stick and the girl—

A: Yeah. I tried to follow them. They're walking down Seventh Avenue, through all the people there, and I'm tryin' to keep up. But you have to be very careful crossin' those streets there 'cause they're asphalt and they rise up in the middle and then if you're not careful you go down the other side too fast and you can't stop and before you know it you crash into the sidewalk, you knock your teeth out on the curb, which around there they have steel rims on them to protect the concrete, which anyway could take more of a beating than my teeth. But I'm tryin' to keep up with them and then they cross Forty-second and get down a ways and the crowds aren't so big there and the spade turns around and sees me. He does that a couple of times, and then he stops and walks back toward me and tells me to get lost. I don't say nothing. I just keep following, and then he talks with the girl and she takes his arm. But he turns around again and tells me to get lost or he'll throw me in the street. I still don't say nothin', but if he comes near me I'm gonna take his foot off.

Then he asks what the fuck I think I'm doin', and I tell him I'm on my way to see my mother. And the girl takes his arm

114

again and they start walkin' again. Then he waves down a cab and they get in, and I'm rollin' fast as I can to get close before they pull away so I can get the plate number. I get the plate number, and I see he's driving Firestone radials. I keep up pretty good. The traffic there on Broadway is bad and it's slowing them down and I could of kept ahead if I'd wanted to.

The spade is watchin' me out the window. He can't figure it out. He thinks I'm crazy.

Then they turn left on Thirty-eighth and the traffic's not so bad and I'm really pushing. I keep catching them at the lights. Then I lose them. So I push fast as I can, staying on Thirty-eighth, and on Third Avenue I see the cab, sitting there empty, and the driver, this hippie kid, waves to me and points into the bar. I look in the bar and I see them and I give this guy at the bar a dime and a phone number and ask him to ask for Martha and tell her to go out and find a kid named Lockley standing around looking lost and tell him where I am. That's a broad works in the Whammy hamburger joint there at Forty-seventh, that's always after me, wantin' a little, you know, and she handles a lot of things for me, takes care of certain things. I know she'll find Lockley and tell him. That's it. I just wait and he shows up, and I split. That's all.

Q: Did you see Lockley the next day?

A: Yeah. Runnin' up the street after the spade.

Q: Before that?

A: No. That was the first I saw him that day.

Q: What did you see then?

A: What I told the cops before. I saw the spade first, runnin' like he's got fire up his ass, without no clothes on, just shorts (laughs), runnin' like black lightning, all legs and arms, with a gun in his hand, and here comes Lockley, runnin' too, and he's got a gun in his hand too. They run up 48th Street, knockin' people down, people standin' there with their big mouths open, starin' like they ain't *never* seen nothin' like this before. That's all.

Q: You ever see Lockley with the Stick before?

A: No. I told you, it was me had to show him who the Stick was. He'd never seen him before.

Q: Or with the girl?

115

A: Lockley with the girl? No. Never. Why? Whaddya think?
Q: Nothing, Joey. Thanks a lot. Where do you want to go?
A: Back to the corner.

TAPE ENDS

[LOCKLEY 6]

I dial the squad, and Schulman answers. I tell him I have to get in touch with Seidensticker. He says he's not there. I say, "Of course he's not there. It's ten o'clock at night. What's his home number?"

"His home number? What's the problem?"

I say, "No problem. He had some girl he wanted me to find, and I found her, so I need—"

Then I hear him yell. "Hey, Castro, Lockley's found a broad for the Owl." And I hear Castro—that's his partner—laughing. They're playing games. I'm standing there going out of my mind to get back to Joey, and they're playing games. "Look," I say, "just give me his number."

"Hang on a second," Schulman says, and then he comes back and he gives me a number. And I call that number and there's no answer. I hang up and I think for a minute. The hell with it. I'm not positive it's Chiclet anyway. I'll watch the loft and call him later.

So I go back to where Joey was, and he's gone. On the sidewalk by the step I was sitting on there's an arrow drawn with a pen, one of his felt pens. An arrow! Pointing toward Seventh Avenue. "Oh, shit," I say, "does he think he's going to leave his tracks with *arrows?*"

I'm standing there huffing and puffing and wondering what to do, looking to where the arrow's pointing, over across the street where there's like a million people milling around, and I'm just about to go over there and start crawling around on the sidewalk looking for arrows when someone behind me says, "Detective Lockley?"

I turn around, and it's a woman. I say, "Yes." It's a heavy, fat old lady with a white uniform.

"I'm from the Whammy," she says. "Someone called for Joey. They said you should meet him at Tudor's Bar, at Thirty-eighth and Third."

"Thanks," I say, and I start looking all around for a cab. No cabs. I look up and down Forty-seventh. Nothing. I run like hell to the corner and look up and down Seventh. No cabs. The traffic is standing still, jammed up as usual, nothing moving, and so if there aren't any empty cabs now, there aren't going to be any.

There's this one cab stopped right in front of me and it's got a man in it reading a paper, and I see an attaché case on the seat next to him, like a commuter going to Penn Station for the Long Island. And I figure, what the hell, he's gonna be late anyway, and I open the cab door and he looks up from his paper and his mouth flies open, and he's really scared. He thinks he's being mugged, right there on Seventh Avenue in a cab in the middle of traffic in front of about a thousand people. It could happen, right? He believes it. The cabbie doesn't say anything. He doesn't even turn around. I show the guy my shield and I say, "I'm a police officer. This is an emergency. You'll have to give me the cab."

And he's re*lieved*. "Of course," he says, and grabs the attaché case and jumps out, trying to hold on to his paper, which is coming all apart and flying around and everything. So I slam the door and I show the shield to the driver and I say, "Thirty-eighth and Third. I've got to be there fifteen minutes ago. Hit the horn and move it."

I'm getting more and more like Crunch all the time now, right? Really learning.

So the driver looks around and takes in the shield, and then he says, "With *pleasure*." And he leans on the horn and pulls out of the left lane, halfway up on the sidewalk, and starts driving like that, half on the sidewalk, half in the street, honking like hell and yelling out the window at the pedestrians he's almost knocking down who are screaming at him.

He was about fifty, and I think it was like a dream come true, like everything he'd ever wanted to do in the traffic, now he can do it and it's all right because he has a cop in the car.

He's pushing the cab around traffic, flashing his lights, honking, yelling, driving on sidewalks, and finally we get to the address.

Joey's on the sidewalk in front of the bar. And I squat down by him and his hands look like Billy's face looked. "I'm sorry," I say. "What happened?"

"I had a helluva time getting here and I lost my boots so I had to push with my hands. But I got here. They're inside."

He had these leather things on his hands for when he pushed along, you know? His hands were really a mess. I gave him my handkerchief and told him I'd try to get him something from the bar. He says the girl and the Stick came out of the loft alone and he followed them on foot—that's what he said, on foot—for a few blocks and then they took a cab. His hands look like hamburger, all bloody, really bad. What balls that guy had. He went from Forty-seventh and Seventh to Thirty-eighth and Third pushing himself with his knuckles practically, and racing a cab most of the way.

So I walk into the place and I sit down at the bar—a huge place, lots of tables, filled with people, mostly hippie types. And in the back at a table in the corner I see the two of them drinking beer, talking, laughing, with a lot of people standing around. I order a beer and sit at the bar, not looking at them, but keeping an eye on them.

And then I walk back to the men's room and I soak some paper towels in hot water and rub soap into them and then I take another stack of dry towels and stuff them in my shirt and walk back through the bar and out to the street and give them to Joey. On the way back from the men's room I'd seen a back door going out from inside the kitchen, so I tell Joey I have to go back because they might leave through the back door, and does he want me to get him a cab, that he should get back and have his hands cleaned good and bandaged. He says no, that he'll wait there for a while and then see what to do. I ask him if he wants to come in and have a beer, and he says no, he doesn't want to do that, just to wait there on the street for a while. I think his hands were really starting to hurt him now that the excitement had worn off. I say okay, that I'll come back out in a few minutes, and I go back in and sit with my beer and watch the Stick and the girl.

She's all over the Stick. Just about everyone in the place is all over him. You couldn't tell who he really knew and who he didn't know because he was like buddies with everybody, laughing and joking and waving. He'd glance at someone and wave and laugh and "Hey, man, how you doin'," and I think half the time it was people he never even saw before. Everyone was watching him, and smiling back, and enjoying him, really. He had this long coat I mentioned before, cut very tight, down to his ankles, and it made him look about eight feet tall. And black leather pants and a black turtleneck, and his hat had a band around it with brass buckles. Some blonde, not Chiclet, one of the people just standing around him, lifted the hat off his head and put it on, and you could see that really bothered him. It didn't turn his big smile off, but it cooled him a little, and he was sort of trying to get the hat back, reaching for it, but not grabbing really, not acting like he wanted it back too bad. He couldn't take his eyes off the hat. And then finally he made a pass at it and got it back and settled down. And after a while the people who were around sucking up to him went back to the bar and the tables, and the Stick and Chiclet just sat there talking.

And by the way, Chiclet was *not* pretty. She was beautiful. Fantastic. These guys like Billy and the Stick, I've got to hand it to them, they get the girls. She was something, really *nice*-looking. She had blue eyes and this long blond hair and she laughed a lot, but not that phony kind of laugh where the girl's just laughing because she thinks she ought to, the way Samantha would probably laugh a lot, but because she really *sees* what's funny, because she's really *happy*. Her whole face was alive, her eyes and her mouth, everything, talking and listening and laughing, just *alive*. It was enough to make me envy the Stick.

So I finish my beer and order another and go out and look for Joey, but he isn't there. I guess he's gone back by himself, but I don't know how he could with those hands. Frankly, I wasn't all that worried about him. I felt sorry for him, because of his hands, that was really bad, but I wasn't worried about him because I figured someone like Joey can always take care of himself.

I drink the beer and keep an eye on Chiclet. And it's really hard not to stare right at her, she's so terrific-looking. And a couple of times I forget and do stare at her and our eyes meet and she looks away. And then I guess she realizes that I'm staring at her, and she starts glancing back at me a lot. And I keep trying not to look at her.

So they have a phone booth in the back and I call Seidensticker's number again, but it doesn't answer. And when I come out of the booth, there she is. She's leaning on the side of the booth, like she's waiting to use it, and she smiles at me and says, "Not home, hunh."

And I say, "No." I can't think of anything else to say. She's going into the booth, and I'm dying for something to say to her, to keep her from going away, but I can't think of anything.

And then she says, "She'll probably be home soon."

So I say, "Oh, it's not that. It's a man."

She kind of raises her eyebrows, pretending to look surprised. She's in the booth now, but just standing there with the door open, and she says, "Who was it?"

And then, just to shock her, and to make sure she doesn't close that door, I do something Crunch would have killed me for. I say, "Your father."

She laughs. This terrific laugh. "My father?" she says.

"That's right," I say, letting her have a piece of very sharp repartee, right?

So she stops laughing then and doesn't get exactly a serious look, she's still smiling, but she isn't playing any more. "What made you say that?"

"Because you're Chiclet."

Then she stops smiling. "Who are you? You're a cop."

And suddenly she bangs the door of the booth and shoves out past me, roughly, and heads back to her table, doesn't look at me or say another word, like I wasn't there. And I see why. The Stick just came out of the men's room and is heading for the table, too.

I go back to the bar and my beer and I sit there trying to figure things out. She goes to the phone, makes a call, comes back and they get up to leave. I run outside, get in a cab and tell the driver to wait a minute, and I slouch down in it so they can't see me. They get in a cab, and I say to the driver, "I want to go where they're going."

"You mean follow that cab?" he says.

"Yeah."

So we follow it and they go to another bar, downtown on

Second Avenue, the East Village, and I give them about five minutes, and then I walk in. And they're in a booth back by the cigarette machine and he's got his arm around her, and he's kissing her. He's got her like curled up in his arm against him, and he's kissing her. I sit down at the bar, and they pull themselves apart a little and she sees me and does a double-take. She gets up and goes to the phone, which is in the back by the rest rooms, in a kind of hallway you can't see into from her table. Then she comes out and goes in the ladies' room.

So I wait a second, and then I go make my call again, still no answer, but I just sit in the booth and let it ring till she comes out of the ladies' room. Then I open the door.

"What are you doing?" she says, not smiling, very annoyed. Annoyed she looks almost as good as when she's laughing.

"Calling your father," I say.

"Listen," she says, "I don't know who you are, but my boyfriend is very jealous and if he finds out you're following me—"

"I'm going to stay with you till this number answers," I say.

She keeps looking up the hall toward the bar and she's getting really nervous. She's scared. She looks at me with these scared eyes, and she says, "Look, I'll see you tomorrow. I can't talk now. We'll both be in a lot of trouble if he sees us. Give me an address and I'll see you tomorrow. Or give me your number and I'll call you."

"Do I look that dumb?"

"I will. I swear I will. You *can't* follow me all night. He'll see you. I swear I'll meet you tomorrow. Honest."

"Where?"

"Across the street. White's. At ten in the morning."

"Okay," I say. "But *be* there. Because if you're not, I can find you again."

"I'll be there," she says, and goes back to the Stick and I leave and go home. And when I get home I call Seidensticker again, and this time he's there. He sounds like he's been at a party, half in the bag, not very pleasant. I say, "I found Chiclet."

He says, "So you found Chiclet. Well, that's beautiful. That's fucking beautiful. And now that you've found her, forget her. You understand? Come in tomorrow on the four-to-twelve.

122

Stay away from her. Lay off her. You never heard of her. You understand?"

I say yes, and he hangs up.

Q: What did you do then?

A: I went to bed. I was tired as hell.

DIERDORF

Sergeant Dierdorf, Det. Butler's SAC contact, was interviewed on tape in the IAD office. Transcription follows.

PRESENT: Capt. Henry Strichter,
Internal Affairs Division

Sgt. Frederick Dierdorf

Q: Let's start with how you became Det. Butler's contact.

A: Capt. D'Angelo thought it was the kind of operation that needed special precautions. He thought we should put her in a SAC, give her a SAC contact.

Q: Why?

A: It's obvious. For the same reason it's used on anybody. Suspicion. I would guess that they thought that with a female undercover and a guy like the Stick, they'd better take all the precautions they could.

Q: Had you had Butler in a SAC before?

A: No. But I knew her. I'd heard about her. I'd talked with her.

Q: How did you feel about her?

A: I didn't like her.

Q: Why?

A: She was a kid. A cocky little kid playing cops and robbers.

Q: Playing it pretty well?

A: She had a lot of luck. She looked like seventeen and when she giggled you'd think she was twelve. She could make it in the schools and on the street with the kids. And with a face like hers, with looking like she did, she had to make good. She couldn't have helped it. Guys were falling over themselves to deal to her.

Q: I've heard she was brave.

A: There's bravery and there's ignorance. She didn't know what she was up against. I've been a SAC contact for six years and I've worked with lots and lots of undercovers, and I've been an undercover for five years myself, and I've seen a lot like Butler. No one can tell them anything. And then someone

126

goes up on them on the street and they get knocked around good and then they're not so cocky any more. There was something about Butler that always rubbed me the wrong way. She just had this attitude, like she was *so* young, like not taking a lot of the other detectives and the supervisors seriously. It was like she was a pretty kid so she could be independent, do everything her way. She thought she had the best way to do everything. She was too young, that's all, just too young. She needed growing up. I didn't trust her, that's all. She was a kid.

Q: So you had this SAC system set up. What if something happened, an emergency, and she had to reach someone in a hurry, did she have a number?

A: Yes. She had a number for me downtown, and she had my home number. She used it that night.

Q: Before we get to that, let me ask you how much you knew about the project she was involved in.

A: Very little. Only what I needed to know. I didn't want to know any more. The SAC system has always been worked on a strict need-to-know basis, and it's saved a lot of problems.

Q: Well, for example, was it your impression that it was her plan to drink and party with the Stick, or to move in with him?

A: I wasn't told. I was just her contact. I was a conduit. My job was to pass information and instructions between Butler and Hanson, and to read her mood and attitude, to watch for signs that something might be going wrong.

Q: Did you know, or do you know now, if she ever met Lockley before this project?

A: I never even heard the name Lockley till that night he found her and she called me.

Q: Did you know if Lockley and the Stick ever had any connection?

A: I told you, I never even knew who this Lockley was.

Q: All right. You were Butler's contact. What happened?

A: I had my first contact with her that Monday, my only contact with her as it turned out. Our days were going to be Monday and Thursday. And then Tuesday night, about midnight, she calls me, and she's in a panic, mad as all hell. She's in a phone booth in a bar, and she says she's been made. I ask her by who. She says she doesn't know, but some kid's been tailing her. She says she was even tailed by a cripple without legs, rolling around on a board with wheels, and she wants to know what's going on. She says she thinks the tail is a cop, and she says she can't shake him, and if he stays with her it's going to be trouble, that someone's going to get hurt. She says to me, "I've got the Stick climbing the walls, eating out of my hand, and this kind of cops-and-robbers bullshit I don't need."

She wants me to tell her what to do. I tell her I don't know any more than she does, which was the truth. I tell her to describe the tail to me. She says the cripple was blond, about twenty-five, that she didn't talk to him, but he had started following her and the Stick at Forty-seventh and Seventh and stayed with them all the way to a bar on Thirty-eighth and Third. She says she spotted the other guy at the bar, good-looking, long hair, about six-foot-two, 180. She says she got a chance to talk to him and he gave her a lot of double talk and she thinks he's a cop.

She says, "I don't care who he is, I want him off, and if he's not off he's gonna get killed." She was giving orders.

I asked her if she could call me back in five minutes. She said she'd try.

I hung up and called Hanson and told him. He said, "Tell her to promise the tail she'll meet him later, get rid of him that way, then call you again in two hours, and after you've done that, get back to me."

She called back, and I told her what Hanson said and then I called Hanson again. He told me he'd just talked to D'Angelo. He told me, "When she calls tell her we know who the tail is and ask if she made a date with him and tell her to ignore him and not see him or talk to him and keep right on like nothing had happened. Tell her don't break her cover, don't tell him anything. Tell her we know all about the tail, and he'll be off her by morning. Tell her that as far as she's concerned, he's off already." He said, "Tell her not to worry about it. It's taken care of."

Q: What did you think about all this?

A: Nothing.

Q: You didn't wonder who the tail was? You didn't ask?

A: I didn't want to know. I found out a long time ago, Captain, just know what you have to know, don't ask questions,

128

and you'll stay out of trouble. I could see this shaping up, and I didn't want any part of it. It looked dirty, and I'd been around long enough to smell dirt and know that it rubs off and that anyone mixed up in this thing was gonna get hurt. I didn't want to know anything. I wanted to get Butler's call and tell her what I had to tell her, and that's all. Period.

Q: What made you so sure it was dirty?

A: Are you kidding? Butler buddying up to a black dealer like the Stick? She had a good record, but she was a con artist, too, and it was pretty obvious to me that this time she'd talked herself in over her head. She'd never been up against someone like the Stick before. He'd teach her what con was. I wanted no part.

Q: You seem pretty hostile.

A: Maybe I am. But with reason.

Q: And not just to Butler and Lockley.

A: I might as well tell you, Captain. I haven't got too much use for the IAD. Things don't work undercover the way they tell you about in the academy. You make your own rules. For an undercover, loyalty can be a weapon, better than a bullet. And these kids in the IAD, loyalty to another cop is something they're told to forget. You pull them right out of the academy and before they even know what it is to be a cop, before they've been on the job a week, you pull them in and tell them that what they're going to be doing is hunting down wrong cops, and they start thinking cops are the bad guys, and the greatest thing they can do is lock up a cop. So when I saw this thing developing I didn't want any part of it. I knew what was going to happen. The bosses all second-guessing. The shoeflies out combing the woods for someone to hang. Tails on everyone. Wires on everyone. That's dirt, Captain. It's dirt.

TAPE ENDS

[HANSON 3]

Q: D'Angelo set it up with the squad commander. And then what happened?

A: I saw D'Angelo and I asked him about it, what had happened with Seidensticker, and he said everything was fine, that he'd just told Seidensticker that there was a runaway thought to be in the Times Square area that they had to go through the motions on. He said he made it sound like a contract, a politician's kid or something like that, and could he spare a man, take him off the chart for a day. He said Seidensticker came on about how short he was on men, and D'Angelo said just anyone at all, and Seidensticker said he did have someone he could spare if it was really important. And he mentioned Lockley. He evidently didn't have too many good things to say about Lockley. And D'Angelo said he told him it didn't matter because it was just a courtesy thing anyway. So that same morning I ran a fast check on Lockley. One look at his performance-evaluation sheets and I figured we had the right man. On paper he looked like the worst detective in the department.

I assigned Sgt. Dierdorf as Butler's contact. Then the next thing I knew I was asleep Tuesday night and Dierdorf called. He said Butler had called him and said she had a tail. I called D'Angelo and got the thing straightened out, and then I called Seidensticker and told him to get Lockley and tell him to forget the girl. If the Stick didn't have the message by now that she was a fugitive, then it wasn't going to happen.

130

[LOCKLEY 7]

I went to bed, and I was shaking. I started coming down from everything, the whole day, and I was thinking about everything, everything at the same time. I thought about Billy and how I'd actually tortured him to tell me where Chiclet was. I thought, now I know how Crunch feels. I hadn't even been that angry at Billy. It was like it just had to be done. It was like asking someone a question but they can't answer you unless you hit them, so you hit them. And then they answer you. I'd never known anything like that before.

And the Stick. If I hadn't minded beating up Billy, I might even have enjoyed beating up the Stick. I couldn't figure why she was with him. I mean if you'd thought of two people in the world who ought *not* to be together, they would have been the two. Everything about him was like he had put it all together so carefully. His clothes and the way he moved and talked and smiled and the way he made his mouth and eyes move, everything was calculated. Like he'd been in training all his life to do what he did. I thought, "She doesn't know what's happening. She won't even know what hits her." Even when he kissed her he kept his eyes open and watched her face, like he knew every little thing that was going on in there, had everything completely under control. I wondered what Crunch would've done about him. That was one collar I wouldn't have minded making. I wouldn't even have minded flaking a guy like that.

I really wanted to be with her. I wanted to talk to her and find out about her. I couldn't stop thinking about her, and about the next morning when I had the date with her in White's. The more I thought about her, the madder I got—I mean at Seiden-sticker and whoever else was involved in this thing. I thought, who the hell do they think they are? I was thinking about what

I'd been through that day, what with the Owl's attitude to begin with, and then the thing with Billy, having to beat the shit out of him, something I never even came close to since I was a kid, and then when I found her and called the Owl and all I get from him is some nasty grunts and a dial tone. I thought about Chiclet some more and how nice she looked, and her eyes when she looked at me by the phone booth, the scared look she had, and about the Stick and what a guy like that might be capable of.

And I figured, fuck 'em. The Owl's telling me, "Lay off her. Forget it." Just like that. Like I'm some piece of shit or something. First it's "Go through the motions, Lockley. Don't break your balls. Have a few beers." And then it's "Forget it. Lay off."

So I'm lying there in bed shaking, with the whole day all rolling around in my head, and I say, "Well, the hell with them. I'm going to White's. My tour doesn't start till four, so if I want to go to White's in the morning, I'll go to White's."

I wanted to talk to her, to find out what it was all about, what she ran away from, why she was with the Stick, if she needed help. I had no faith in the PD to give her any help *at all*.

So finally I slept for a couple of hours, and then I got up and dressed and put on the ankle holster. I was getting used to it. Why not?

And at 9:30 I'm in White's. With all the winos, right? At 9:30?

At 10:30 I know she's not coming, but I wait till noon anyway. For another hour and a half I'm sitting there drinking beer and waiting. And while I'm waiting, I'm thinking did she stand me up, or did something happen to her. When she made the date, I'd really believed her. Maybe I shouldn't have, but sometimes you just believe people even when it looks like you shouldn't. And thinking about how frightened she'd looked, and being with a guy like the Stick, I started worrying about her. I'd worry and then I'd think, "No, she's okay, she just stood you up." And then I'd get pissed off because she stood me up, and I'd be sore for a while, and then I'd think, "But maybe she's really in trouble, maybe she couldn't come," and then I'd get worried again and start all over. And then eventually I decided, well, whichever way it is, I'm going to find out. I'm not going to just walk out of here and fade away like some jerk, just go back and do my four-to-twelve like nothing had happened.

So I go back to Forty-seventh and Seventh, to the Stick's loft. It's about 12:30 now, I guess. And I stand across the street, where I was with Joey the night before, and I watch the building for a while, and no one goes in or out. So I walk across the street and I go in the hall and I look at the boxes. The box for the fourth floor hasn't got any name on it at all. I start up the stairs.

On the fourth floor there's just one door, this heavy steel black door. I ring the bell, and then I move back on the stairs out of sight. And I hear the door open, and some guy says, "Shit," and I hear Chiclet yelling at him, something, I couldn't hear what, but really yelling at him. He doesn't say anything, and then I hear her very close, like right behind him in the door, and then some water, or some kind of liquid, comes flying out the door, like she'd thrown a glass of water at him or something, and he yells and laughs and I hear him chasing her back into the apartment. And then I hear the door scrape, just scrape closed against the jamb.

I come out from the stairs, and I push the door open. I can hear Chiclet and the Stick yelling in the back. I don't know if they're fighting or playing or what. I go inside and pull the door to behind me. I was scared as hell. No. I wasn't scared. I was excited. My heart was pounding, and all that, and I wasn't thinking. I was just doing what I was doing. Right now I couldn't tell you for certain why I went in that loft. Maybe I wanted to make sure Chiclet was all right. But I don't really know. At the time it just seemed like—I didn't even think of *not* going in. I mean, it wasn't, "Should I go in or not. If I go in, this might happen, and if I don't go in, that might happen." I was just *going* to go in.

So I'm in and I can hear the Stick and Chiclet talking somewhere way, way in the back. And this loft isn't just one huge room any more, like when it was a dance studio or the discothèque. It's been divided up, and walls put in, and the hall I'm in now is very small, with about four doors. And I look through one and I see this—like a printing plant. There's three mimeographing machines, and some other machine, and stacks of paper still wrapped up and tables covered with paper. I go in there, and then I hear the Stick out in the hall again, locking the front door. Then I hear him walking back to the back of the apartment and I hear him and Chiclet talking together, only I can't make out what they're saying. I go back out to the hall and I look through this other door and I see a wooden crate on the floor, with a top pulled off, and all around it are guns, hand guns, pistols. And there's like a workbench over on one side, and tools on it and some parts of guns.

I'm standing there in this gun room trying to take it all in, and now their voices stop and I hear footsteps, just someone moving around way in the back there. Then I don't hear anything for a while, and then I hear the Stick call something from one side of the apartment back there and then some walking around and then both their voices together again softer, and then no sound at all. So I move over to a door on the far side of this gun room and I go through and I'm in a hall, and at the end of the hall there's another door.

Now all of a sudden I hear something fall, like a chair or a lamp or something falling, on the other side of the door, and then I hear laughing, very clearly, right on the other side of that door, and I'm just thinking that this is a good time to get the hell out of here when the door flies open and it's her.

She's completely naked, and when she opens the door she's looking back at him, laughing, and starts through the door without seeing me. Then she turns her head around and sees me, and her face drops and she stops, and she just stands there frozen.

Then he comes into the doorway, in his shorts, and he sees me, and right away, like a reflex, he turns around and runs back into the room.

I run up to the door now, because of the way he looked, and the hurry he was in, and I was scared what he was doing. Because a guy like the Stick, the things he's into, with a flat full of guns, he's not going to mess around when he sees some strange guy in his apartment, right? He's gotta assume right off he's in trouble—someone's gonna take him off, or hit him, or whatever, and he's not gonna be looking to conduct an investigation.

I yell, "I'm a cop!" And that has no effect at all. Like even if he believes me, he's got as much to worry about from cops as from anyone else. So I go in and I see him next to the bed, trying to open the drawer of the table there, and I drop down on one knee and try to get the gun out of my ankle holster.

I'm having as much trouble with my cuff and my sock as he's having with the drawer. Then the drawer comes open and his hand comes out of it with a piece and right then there's this like just a blur and Chiclet is flying at him.

And now you've got to remember that all this happened in about half a second. And Chiclet is flying at him, I guess trying to knock the gun away, and she hits him with her body and I get my piece out and he pushes her away across him, down onto the bed, and as he does this he opens fire, and I shoot back, neither of us aiming. And he's just standing there next to the bed with one arm holding Chiclet down and I'm on my knees, and we both fire about two shots at each other, and then he makes a dive for the window and drops down about five feet to a setback, and I go after him. I chase him across the setback, about ten or fifteen yards, through all these clotheslines and clothes hanging on them, and then through a window into the stairwell of a hotel there, and down about four flights of stairs.

I wasn't thinking anything at all, I was just taking those stairs like mad, and all the way down the stairs I'm gaining on him, like a step a floor, and then we're at the bottom and he pounds through the door out to 48th Street and he runs to Sixth Avenue, crosses Sixth, and just keeps going.

And he's knocking people down all over the place. It's about one o'clock, something like that, and everyone's out for lunch and he's running right over people, and I'm right behind him. And I mean I'm *really* right behind him, because this guy tried to kill me, right? Attempted murder! Not to mention the guns and whatever else a good toss would turn up in that apartment.

So I chase him all the way over to Fifth Avenue, and he makes a left. And I'm winded as hell now, but I know he is, too, and I'm wondering where are all the cops on post. Here are two guys with drawn guns, one in his shorts, running up Fifth Avenue, knocking people over, running like they've just robbed a bank or something, and no cop anywhere doing anything.

So he gets right in front of Saks, at 50th Street, and people are pouring in and out of the revolving doors, and he stops and dashes for this little side door, next to the revolving doors, and he pushes through it and I follow him, and he's running up the aisle and people are flying left and right, and then he gets by the elevators and he stops and turns around and levels his gun at me and I stop, too, and bring mine up at him.

And just then, before either of us can do anything, an elevator arrives and the people inside don't know anything, of course, about what's going on here, but the door opens and when they start coming out, the first ones see us with guns drawn and an old man screams and runs like hell and then everyone on that elevator just cleared out in a second like it was on fire.

So we're standing there, guns on each other, and all these people, these shoppers, are going crazy all around us, running and screaming, trying to get out of the way. And I can't shoot because of this mob, and the Stick, he doesn't take the time to shoot, he makes a wild dash for the elevator and dives into it, and I dive in after him. And he's going so fast, his momentum throws him against the elevator wall and I slam in against him and the door closes, and he pulls himself off the wall and straightens up with the gun on me, and I sort of drop down, slump down, and I have my gun on him, and there we are, the elevator going up and both of us about three feet away from each other with our guns pointed at each other's bellies.

BLACKSTONE

Two days after his conversation with Lieutenant Lyon in the Topper bar, Detective Blackstone was called to the Internal Affairs Division office and interviewed by Captain Strichter. Transcription follows.

PRESENT: Capt. Henry Strichter,
  Internal Affairs Division

Det. Richard Blackstone

[BLACKSTONE 4]

Q: Tell me what happened the Wednesday of the homicide.

A: I was in the squad room with Schulman, typing, and I heard a Shots Fired over the radio, on 48th Street. I stopped typing and Schulman and I were listening, and then about half a minute later there was a Signal 13 at Fiftieth and Fifth, and Schulman and I looked at each other, and got up and got in the car and went over.

At Sixth and Forty-eighth I saw this guy without any legs who sells pencils around there talking to a patrolman. I waited until they were finished and the pencil guy left and then I asked the cop what he said. The cop told me that the pencil fellow had said he saw two men with drawn guns running toward Fifth and that he knew them and that one was called the Stick and the other was Detective Lockley. I knew the Stick. He was a very bad kid. Very dangerous. I'd talked to him a few times, and we knew each other. I was looking to hand him a collar, and he knew it, and we had one of those kind of things, you know what I mean, where we'd see each other on the street and talk a couple of minutes and maybe have a laugh, and we both knew sooner or later we were gonna be up on each other.

Schulman and I went to find the pencil guy and he said the Stick lived in a flat on Forty-seventh, and he pointed it out to us.

Schulman and I went up. Some flat. Rooms all over the place, a converted loft, filled with guns, printing equipment, books. And Schulman was looking it over and I walked through a hallway into a bedroom and to the right of the door when I went in I saw a girl lying by a bed, naked, half on the bed, half off —her head and chest on the bed, but the rest of her body hang-

138

ing over. And I recognized her. I'd seen her on the street and I thought she was a junkie. I called Schulman in and I felt her pulse and there wasn't any. There was quite a lot of blood on the bed and on the floor around her. I told Schulman to call the M.E. and the squad and to stay there, and I went back out to the street and over to Fiftieth and Fifth where the Assist Patrolman had come from.

Q: What time was it then?

A: Just before two. A couple of minutes. When I got to Fifth I saw all the cars in front of Saks, and a cop told me Lieutenant Seidensticker was inside with the captain. I went in and they were up on the sixth floor standing in front of an elevator bank, and I told them what I'd found in the flat, and that it looked like the men with the guns were Lockley and the Stick, and that I knew the Stick, that he was a dangerous kid.

Seidensticker told me they'd gone into an elevator and that the elevator was stopped between the fifth and sixth floors. They had a man from the store trying to open a control panel next to the elevators.

Seidensticker asked me did I know who the girl was. I said some junkie I'd seen around the precinct, but that I hadn't taken time to check out the apartment. I said she looked in her late teens, a nice build. Schulman came up then and said detectives from the squad and homicide were in the apartment, and that one of them recognized the girl as a narcotics undercover named Pat Butler. Seidensticker gave him some look. Schulman almost backed up, like it was his fault.

Seidensticker said, "Is he *sure?*"

"He says he's been with her on jobs, knows her as well as his partner," Schulman said.

Seidensticker asked a man from the store where he could find a phone, and the guy took him into the buyer's office, and I went with them. Seidensticker called Chief Perna of the Narcotics Bureau and told him it looked like one of his undercovers was dead in an apartment on 47th Street, and that it looked like she was shot either by a black dealer known as the Stick or by a detective named Lockley. He told Perna that the Stick and Lockley were together in an elevator. Perna said he was coming over.

[HANSON 4]

Then the next afternoon, Wednesday afternoon at about 2:15, Chief Perna called me into his office, and as soon as I walked in and saw D'Angelo there and looked at their faces, I knew—something, something really bad. D'Angelo looked like a piece of stone, and Perna was standing up, putting on his jacket. Perna said he'd just had a call that Butler had been killed. He said a cop and a dealer who were apparently involved were in an elevator on Fifth Avenue. I can't tell you how I felt. I was—like someone had just slugged me in the stomach. I looked at D'Angelo. He was staring straight at Perna, all tightened up, trying to keep hold of himself.

Perna said, "Before we go up there, I want to know everything you know about what happened."

Then D'Angelo looked at me.

Perna said, "Hanson, you're her supervisor. What was she doing?"

I said, "She's been working a dealer who just moved downtown. His name's Thomas Henderson, a/k/a the Stick. She asked permission to work him exclusively for a couple of weeks. I checked his CIB background and it looked promising and I gave her permission."

Then D'Angelo said, "We discussed it, Chief. Hanson came to me. We both talked to Butler and went over the CIB file and we okayed it. It didn't look like any special problems."

Perna didn't even take time to react to that. He said, "We'll talk about that later. You sure that's all you know?"

I said, "Well, there were details, but basically that's it."

My guess, to tell you the truth, knowing Perna and the way things work, I'd say that at that moment he didn't want to know any more. He was waiting to see how things developed. He

140

wanted the rough outline of what it was about, I mean he didn't
want it to look like he didn't know what was going on in his
command, but on the other hand if something wrong was going
on, he didn't want to hear anything where later he might have
to deny he knew it. I think he wanted to be sure about what
was up at Saks before he jumped in.

So we drove up to Saks, Perna, D'Angelo and me, and when
we got there the place looked like an armed camp. Seidensticker
was there, and Sgt. Dierdorf, Butler's contact. Seidensticker
briefed us. He said Butler was dead in an apartment that had
been occupied by the Stick, and that evidently Lockley had
chased the Stick into the elevator and that they were at an im-
passe in there. He said he'd sent for an engineer from Otis.

Then Perna asked if there was an office with a phone, and
a cop showed him one and Perna took D'Angelo and me in
with him. Only he didn't want a phone, he wanted to get away
from Seidensticker and the others and talk to us. He sat down
behind a desk in this office and he looked hard at D'Angelo
and he said, "Johnny, I want to know what this is all about. I
want to know it all. Right now. If you and Hanson get jammed
up in this thing, I'm going to have to go with you because I'm
your boss. And I'm not getting jammed up if I can help it."

That was the spot Perna was in. Like the Navy—the navigator
runs the ship aground, the captain gets hung. Perna was trying to be calm, but it was taking quite an effort. He said, "If
there's more to this, tell me now. I don't want any surprises.
Tell me now and maybe we can try to work something out."

Perna and D'Angelo just stared at each other then, for a
long time, like Perna was going to sit there all day until D'Angelo came across, and D'Angelo was thinking fast, should he
risk giving the whole thing up or not.

Then D'Angelo said, "We told you everything, Chief. It's
like we said. The only thing more to it is that we thought it'd
be a good idea to do something to reinforce her position with
the Stick. We discussed an idea with her and she went for it."
Then he gave him the rough outlines of Lockley's role. Perna
just listened, didn't react at all.

"That's it?" Perna said. "All of it?"

"All of it," D'Angelo said.

And that was the end of that conversation.

We went back to Seidensticker and the captain and this mob of people trying to decide what to do. Perna was senior officer present, and he started asking for ideas about how to get the Stick and Lockley out of the elevator. And everyone was suggesting things, like getting the Stick's relatives to come down, talking stuff to him, threatening him, talking nice, promising things, waiting it out, starving him out.

D'Angelo wanted to end it quickly. He could see, as we all could, that it was going to develop into a real operation, and he wanted to end it fast, to open the elevator doors and take them out, regardless of the consequences.

Q: What did Chief Perna say?

A: He said he wanted to exhaust every other possibility before he did anything like that.

[LOCKLEY 8]

So we're in there with our guns on each other and the elevator going up, and then the Stick reaches out and presses the stop button and we jerk to a stop. I figure he thinks that when the elevator gets to wherever it's going, the door will open again and he's gonna be trapped by a mob of shoppers. So he decides to stop. Which is the worst mistake he ever made, but probably lucky as hell for the people waiting for the elevator.

So there we are, in a standoff. If I do anything he'll blow my insides out, and if he does anything I'll blow his insides out. I know that even if I shoot him in the head he's gonna have one last reflex to pull the trigger. And how can he miss? The muzzle of his gun is practically touching my stomach. We're both panting like dogs, really exhausted from all the running. And he's looking all around the elevator, and I can tell he's wondering what he got himself into, if he did the right thing coming in the elevator, and then again if he did the right thing stopping it.

And I'm thinking, as soon as this guy has a second to go over the kind of trouble he's in, he's going to get very, very desperate. He'll figure it out fast. By now the cops have torn up his apartment and found the guns and whatever else there is, drugs or whatever. Plus he threw shots at me, so that's attempted murder of a police officer. So with whatever kind of sheet he's got, he'll be looking into so many years he'll die in prison. Whether he kills me or not, he'll die in prison.

I look up and I see the floor indicator is lighted at five, which means we could be anywhere between four and six. Then the Stick gets some of his breath back and leans back against the wall and then slides down till he's sitting, and I get into a sitting position against the opposite wall, and we're both there with our

143

backs against opposite walls, our legs stretched out, guns on each other.

Then he says, "Who the hell are you?"

"A friend of Chiclet's."

"A friend of Chiclet's," he says, looking me over. "How'd you find that apartment?"

"I just found it." He sits there, trying to get things together. "What are you going to do?" I say.

"Well, it looks a little heavy, don't it," he says. "I don't know. But whatever happens, I got company. Don't I?"

"I guess you do. Why not surrender?"

"Surrender? To you? You *really* a cop? Man, you'd like that collar. Get a promotion."

"What are you going to do if you don't give up?"

"Well," he says, "maybe I'll just press that button again and ride down and get out and walk back to the house."

"I think that by now you'd encounter a little opposition."

"You do?" he says. "You do for sure? Encounter a little opposition?"

Then we just sit there. I look at my watch and it's 1:30. I figure we've been there about fifteen minutes. I can imagine the scene outside. About a million radio cars all over Fifth Avenue, and all the cops in the world. So what's going to happen, I ask myself. What should I be doing? I wonder how long it's going to take them to find out who's in here, and I wonder what the Stick's plan, when he figures one out—and he is over there deep in thought—will be. And what I ought to do.

"I think we're gettin' out of here," he says, and stands up with the gun still on me, always with the gun on me, and mine on him.

"What the hell are you doing?" I ask him.

"I'm gettin' out of here."

"The store's loaded with cops by now," I say. "They're not going to let you go anywhere."

"They are if you're with me. 'Cause if they don't let me out, they can't let you out. And if you're a cop, I know they'll want you out. And to get you, they got to let me out and give me a car and stand back, because you're gonna be right there with me."

"Wrong," I say. "I'm not your hostage." I wave my gun a

little. "We are each other's hostages. We do nothing except by agreement. If they open that door and you try to go out with me as a hostage, I'm not moving. I'm sitting right here. And there's nothing you can do to get me up. You fire one shot and you're dead."

He nods his head a few times. Then he sits down and he goes back to the old drawing board, thinking hard as hell. And I think about his hostage plan, and a thought comes to me. There's an intercom in the elevator, and if he uses it and tells the cops outside that he's got someone with him, and they know he's not lying, that he really *does* have a hostage, and a cop at that, then where does that put them? What can they do? They can't move.

On the other hand, if he tells them he's got a hostage, and can't *prove* it, what about that? Because if he was here alone, the most natural thing would be for him to make up a story about how he had a hostage with him, right? But if he can't make the cops buy it, it's no good. For it to work, they've got to *believe* it. If they believe he's got a hostage, he has the initiative and they can't make a move. But if he can't prove he's got a hostage, and they think he's lying, then they've got the initiative and they can do what they want, and it'll be like he didn't have a hostage at all.

So that seems like a pretty cool revelation to me. And I think it over and I examine it closely and I decide that if I don't talk, if I don't say anything, and they can't hear my voice over that intercom, how else is the Stick going to prove I'm here? All he can do is describe how I'm dressed and what I look like, but that could be a million guys. And even if he figures, well, someone had to remember the two guys running into the elevator, he can't be *sure* the cops will go along with the confused recollections of some panicked shoppers. So all I've got to do is keep my mouth shut, and any hostage plans he comes up with aren't going to be worth a damn. I hope.

Of course, if the cops really think he's alone in here, they might just decide to open the doors and come in shooting. But I don't think they'll do that. I think that before they do that they'll be pretty damn sure who's in this elevator. As far as the Stick's concerned, the cops can play it dumb and say he's full

145

of shit, that they don't believe he's got anyone, and then what's he going to do? Where's his hostage then?

So we just sit there, neither of us saying anything, both trying to figure out what to do. And we sit there for a long time, and then we hear the intercom go on, just background noise at first and then we hear, "In the elevator! Can you hear me?"

And the Stick is on his feet like a shot. The intercom shook him up. I don't think he knew it was there. "Yeah, man," he says. "I hear you."

"This is Captain Whalen of the 16th precinct. Your elevator is between floors. We are going to raise it to the sixth floor. Then we will open the doors and I want you to throw your gun out of the elevator and then on our instructions take three steps out of the elevator into the aisle. Do you understand that?"

The Stick hits his fist on the wall. He sticks his mouth right up against the intercom speaker and he shouts, "I understand, pig. But it ain't gonna happen. I've got a pig in here with me, one of your finest detective pigs, and if this elevator moves, he's *dead*. You understand *that?*"

There's no answer. The background noise goes off and it's dead. The Stick steadies his gun at me. "If they move this here elevator one inch," he says, "I'm gonna blow your motherfuckin' guts out."

I level my piece at his belly, and shrug. But I want to tell you, I was scared absolutely shitless.

About half an hour or so after that, the intercom comes on again and the captain says, "In the elevator! Identify yourself. If you've got a police officer in there, let me talk to him."

"I'll identify myself, you motherfuckin' pig. I'm Thomas Robert Henderson, and you move this elevator one inch and your pig in here is dead. You wanna talk to him, talk to him . . ."

He looks down at me, and makes a motion to the speaker with his hand, like I should stand up and say a few words. I shake my head. "Come on, man," he says, "talk to the man."

I just sit there, with my gun on his belly. Then he begins to see it. "Get up here, man, and talk into this thing or I'll blow your motherfuckin' head off."

And he puts the piece about a foot from my head. I raise my arm and reach out and just touch the muzzle of my gun to the skin over the top of his shorts. I've just about got it stuck into his navel.

"Henderson? Let me talk to whoever you've got in there!"

He tilts his head toward the intercom, keeping an eye on me and keeping his piece at my head. "In just about one minute, pig. Call me back in a minute."

The intercom stays on, you can hear the noise from it, and in fact it stayed on the whole time now, it never went off again. And the Stick sits down and lowers the piece a bit and says to me, "You crazy, man? Why don't you speak to your pig leader out there?"

I shake my head.

"Listen, you lose your voice, or what? Why don't you want to speak to him?"

But of course he knows why. And he's mad as hell at himself now for saying something to me before about using me to get out and get a car and all that. Then he stands up again and yells at the speaker. "You hear me out there?"

"We hear you."

"Your buddy in here just lost his voice. He don't want to talk none. But he's here, you'd better believe it, and if you try to move this here elevator or open the doors he's gonna die and I don't care if I go with him or not. You understand that? So here's what I want. I want a piece of paper from the mayor on the mayor's stationery from City Hall saying I won't be prosecuted for nothing that happened today. I want that signed from the mayor on his own stationery. You understand? And I want the same thing from the DA. Same promise. Then I throw out the gun. You got that?"

"We hear you."

He waits by the intercom for about a minute, then he yells, "Well? What you say?"

"I said we hear you."

He sits down again, and I guess outside they're mulling over that mild little request and figuring what to do. So we just sit there. It's about a quarter of four now. We've been there since 1:15, about two and a half hours. And I'm just beginning to feel a little cramped, my knees are feeling like they want moving and bending, but I'm afraid to do anything except concentrate on keeping my piece steadied at the Stick. Because I *know* that if he sees I'm not paying attention and he thinks he can grab the piece, he's going to do it, and then he's got me and I'm *really* in trouble, because then there's no telling what crazy demands he'll make, planes to Cuba, or Algeria, all that, everything.

Anyway, we sit there for a long time, and then he gets up again and yells at the intercom, "You out there?"

"Oh, yes. We're out here." It's still the captain talking.

"I made you an offer, man, and I ain't heard nothin' back."

"You call that an offer, Henderson? You know we can't make promises like that. You know the mayor and the DA can't buy that. The only way you're going to get out of there is if you do what I told you to do and throw out your gun when the doors open, and walk out."

He got really upset when the captain mentioned the doors opening. "Those doors'd better not open, pig. 'Cause the minute they start openin', your man in here is dead. You get me? *Dead!*"

He really yelled. He was terrified of them opening the doors. I'm sure he knew the kind of firepower they had out there by now and he thought once the doors opened he was as good as assassinated.

"Stop trying to tell us you've got someone in there, Henderson," the captain says.

Now the Stick's really disturbed. Not just mad, but upset, frustrated. "You think I'm bluffin'," he yells at the intercom, "then you just open them doors and take a look and you're gonna see one motherfuckin' pig detective or whoever he is blown all over this here elevator. You want to see that, then you call my bluff, you just call it."

Well, there's no answer to that. The Stick sits back down, and I stop thinking what I'd been thinking. Because for the last few seconds, maybe a minute, he'd been so fired up and his mind was so occupied with the captain outside and what he was yelling that I could see he wasn't thinking about his gun. When he talked he gestured with his hands, and the piece moved around a lot, and it wasn't always right on me. And I thought I could probably grab it, or I could fire a shot into his head and then grab it and hold it till he couldn't do anything.

I *thought* I could do that, I mean that it would be *possible* to do that, but I didn't have the nerve. I just couldn't do it.

Then when he's calmed down a little and sitting down again, I say to myself, "You were really stupid, you coward. It could have been all over, and now you don't know what's going to happen, how it's going to come out, and you might be the one who ends up dead." So I decide if I get another chance like that I'm going to take it.

"He wants to call my bluff, he's gonna have somethin' to see," the Stick says. He's talking as much to himself as to me. Then he looks up at me and points the gun right at my head, and he snarls, really *snarls,* and he says, "You think you're a smart motherfucker, don't you. But the only way you're gonna get out of this with your head still on is if you tell them you're here with me. 'Cause if they *don't* think you're here with me, they're gonna blow this whole elevator away."

[HANSON 5]

There was a lot of conversation over the elevator intercom with the Stick. Lockley was behaving very intelligently, refusing to confirm his presence. And the captain was smart, too, not telling Henderson anything, just playing it dumb, as if he didn't have any idea in the world who was in the elevator.

Every time anyone did anything or suggested anything, D'Angelo became more and more impatient. He wanted to put a stop to things—immediately, by any means. He was convinced that the amount of trouble for all of us would be in direct proportion to the amount of time the Stick was in the elevator. He was even trying to convince Perna and me that maybe Lockley wasn't really in the elevator. That lost him some strength with Perna. Perna doesn't like to be conned.

[LOCKLEY 9]

I think about that for a while, that they might just blast away at the elevator. I can *tell* you I thought about that. And I know it's probably true. They might. If they don't know I'm here. But I'm sure they'll figure out I *am* here, and why I'm keeping quiet. Only even when you're sure, in a situation like that—well, just *sure* isn't enough, you understand? I keep going over it in my mind, all the ways they can't help but know I'm here. All the people who must have seen me chasing the Stick. Chiclet— would Chiclet tell them I was chasing him? Why wouldn't she? Of course she would. Maybe they could tell some way from the elevator's weight that there are two people in it. There must be about a million detectives assigned to this by now, and some of them have got to be smart enough to figure out something. Then I hear the Owl.

"Henderson!"

He stands up. "Yeah."

"This is Lieutenant Seidensticker of the 16th squad."

"Seiden-*what?*"

"Seidensticker, squad commander of the 16th squad. You say you've got one of my men in there with you, but it's futile of you to say that because we've just run a check and every member of the squad is accounted for."

Now *that's* not dumb. Now I know they know I'm here, right?

"Man, I didn't say I had one of your men in here. I said I got a guy I think is a pig, a guy who said he's a pig. I don't know what kind of pig, man, maybe your pig, maybe a narco pig, maybe anything, man, maybe he's just a somebody and he ain't a pig at all, but *I* think he is." He glances down at me. "He looks like one." First time anyone said that about me.

151

That conversation ends, and we're just sitting again. And now it's beginning to smell. The store is air-conditioned and there's air blowing in through some louvers in the ceiling, but it's not enough. We've been there almost four hours now, and we're both sweating like hell, there's sweat dripping down the Stick's forehead, and his chest and stomach are all wet with sweat. And my shirt is just about soaked. And it stinks like hell. And I'm still cramped. And I'm tired of having to think about the piece in my hand all the time, always to keep it leveled at him, and never to let it look like my mind is off it. Because I know if he ever gets a chance like the one he gave me, I've had it. And I'm worried about my father and mother. I wonder if they have my father out there. I'm worried about what this is doing to them.

We sit for about an hour then, leaning up against the walls, and then the Stick says, "They so sure you ain't here, how come they don't open the doors?"

I shrug. He sort of snorts and makes a laugh. "We're just gonna sit here then forever, man, till they decide to give me those papers. Otherwise, we'll sit here till we starve to death."

Another half hour or so and we hear the captain's voice.

"Henderson!"

He doesn't stand up. He's sitting with his knees up, the piece in both hands between his knees. "I ain't gone nowhere," he says.

"We've got someone who wants to talk to you. We've explained the situation to her—"

That turned us both on. Chiclet, right?

"We've told her the situation you're in and we've told her the demands you've made and how futile they are. She wants to talk to you."

Silence for a few seconds, and then a woman's voice, but not Chiclet's.

And then the Stick groans. "Oh, *man* . . ."

[BLACKSTONE 5]

Q: What was going on with the elevator all this time?

A: All this time they're trying to get into the elevator control panel, and then someone had called Otis and one of their engineers came over and they all checked in around the controls for a while with the captain and some detectives about what they could do with the elevator, could they move it, could they open the outer doors. And the Otis man said there was an intercom and they could talk to whoever was in the elevator if they wanted to. The captain takes the telephone and he gets the Stick on the other end and he tells him he's going to raise the elevator to the floor and for him to come out. The Stick says forget it, that he's got a hostage, a cop. The captain doesn't know what to say behind that because he doesn't want to tell the Stick anything, to admit that he knows Lockley is in there, or not admit it, either. He hands the phone back to the Otis man and everyone talks it over. The captain says the one thing he wants for sure is to keep the elevator where it is, not have it start moving all over the store from floor to floor. The Otis man says that's easy and he does something to disconnect the buttons inside the elevator so they couldn't control it.

All the brass starts arriving. Chief Perna, Captain D'Angelo, Lieutenant Hanson. Do they look worried! One of their people killed, heads are gonna roll. Perna a year away from retirement, and D'Angelo and Hanson still tryin' to claw their way onward and upward. None of 'em been on the street in years and years. Just pushing paper and worryin'—who's got this squad, who's got that squad, who's gettin' this division, that division, who's got the biggest hook, who's movin' up, who's gettin' flopped. Man, that's a full-time job. That's a whole career all by itself. And now ol' Lockley, he's got 'em jammed up good. You shoulda

153

seen 'em. Scared, man. Much as I hated the whole thing, especially about Butler, it did something for me, I have to admit it, to see those bosses lookin' so downhearted. They really caught one this time. This time they're in the street, right out in the middle, and in come the vests and the artillery, and there ain't no side-steppin' now, no sir, just cops, everyone out there naked in front of everyone.

And then the stuff starts moving in in force. A guy from Emergency Service comes up to D'Angelo and asks him, "What do you want? Shotguns or Thompsons." And D'Angelo, of course, being D'Angelo, says, "Everything, bring in everything."

About six carloads of cops are there already, plus Emergency Service, and now a lot of other cops are pouring in and they're lugging in helmets and bulletproof vests and it's turning into one of those full-scale productions.

First off, Perna sees a couple of civilians walking around and gets pissed off. The uniformed men have been trying to empty out the store, but there's still a few stragglers left, and Perna orders the captain to get the store emptied out fast, which the captain of course has been tryin' to do anyway for about an hour. Then the captain gets back on the phone to the elevator and he tries to get the Stick to prove that he's got someone in there with him, to let him hear the other guy talk. But Lockley begins to show he's not dumb. We don't hear anything. We hear the Stick talking in there, but we don't hear anything from Lockley.

Off and on, for the next few hours, they're talking with the Stick, telling him they're gonna open the doors, and he's saying if they do he'll kill his hostage. And I thought we ought to do something to let poor old Lockley know we understand. Like he was smart enough to keep his mouth shut, we ought to let him know we know he's there so he won't have a nervous breakdown worryin' about us firing shots into the elevator. Seidensticker has the idea the same time I do, and he says that if he goes on the phone, then Lockley will know what the score is. And he does that.

We've let Lockley in that we know he's there, but still we're not getting any place. Like they say, the status is quo. People start throwing ideas around. D'Angelo from the start is crazy. He's pissed about Butler, which is certainly understandable, we all are. But what he wants, his idea, is to shoot it out, open the door and shoot it out. A couple of people jump on him for that. I let myself be heard. And Hanson, he gives it to him good. D'Angelo tries to say how do we know Lockley's there, maybe the Stick *is* bluffing. Hanson says, well, if he isn't there, where is he, and anyway we have interviews by then with customers and a salesgirl who saw two men run into the elevator, one right after the other, both of them with guns. It isn't all that hard to figure out the situation in there, both of them with guns. But D'Angelo wants to blast away. He's getting his rocks off, you know what I mean? He's back out from behind his desk, playin' with the big boys now, and he's showin' everyone how tough he is, what a man he is. Let's go to war, let's blast the shit out of that elevator.

This was when I started thinking about what was my responsibility. To Lockley, I mean. I was the only one there who really knew him, as much I mean as anyone knew him, because Perna and D'Angelo didn't know him at all. Even to Seidensticker he was just another detective in the squad, and all he knew about him was that he was a problem. But I was one of Lockley's partners, you know what I mean? We'd been on the street together, and like no one there was thinking about him. I knew that. Lockley was a problem now, the situation he'd got himself into was a problem, and they were all thinkin' real hard about the *problem*. But they wasn't thinkin' about Lockley. And like I say, I started to think some about what I should do. I could see what was shaping up. D'Angelo wanted to blast. The only one keeping him from it was Perna. Perna's smart, he's cool, he's more levelheaded than D'Angelo. He was thinking everything through, and as long as blasting stood to make more of a problem than not blasting, Perna was gonna be very sharp and cute and keep D'Angelo in check, and there wouldn't be no blasting.

But things were gonna get rough, almost anyone could see that. The Stick wasn't gonna give up and come out. Not with what he had behind him. Not the Stick. He'd die in there first. And you know they can't let him stay in there forever. It's gonna get rough. Perna is gonna have to move closer and closer to D'Angelo's point of view, to blast and end it. Like I say, I was

155

thinking about this and trying to get a set on my place, what my responsibilities were.

Then we get a report from CIB that the Stick has a mother living uptown on 112th Street, and Perna orders a car up there to get her. She comes down, and Perna puts her on the phone. Like the Stick's gonna be a good boy and come out because his mother tells him to. Perna watches too much television.

[LOCKLEY 10]

The second the Stick hears his mother's voice, he jumps up and he looks like he'd kill the whole world right then and there.

"Tommy, the officers say you're in there and you got a gun and there ain't nothin' you can do but come on out. They promise they ain't gonna hurt you, Tommy, but you got to come on out. You got to come out, Tommy, or somethin' terrible—"

Her voice starts to break. It's all the Stick can do to keep his eyes on me.

"—Or somethin' terrible gonna happen. Please come out, Tommy. I ain't never asked you nothin', but please tell them you'll come on out."

"That's your mother, Henderson," the captain says. "She's giving you good advice. You'd better—"

Now the Stick screams. "I *know* it's my mother, you motherfuckin' pig!"

"She's hearing you, Henderson."

"Mama," the Stick says. "Go home, Mama. You don't understand what they're doin'. Go home. You don't understand."

Then we hear another voice.

"Henderson, this is Chief Perna of the Narcotics Bureau. We know you haven't got anyone in there with you and it's stupid and useless to keep telling us you have. You can't stay in there forever. You're going to have to come out. If you come out now, we'll do everything we can to see that you get the best possible deal with the DA. We'll do our best. We can't make promises, and you know it. But we'll try. You're going to have to come out sometime, Henderson, one way or another, and it'll be better for you to come out now than later. Do you understand?"

"I understand, pig, and my answer is the same. I don't care

157

how many pig big shots come over this phone. It don't change nothin'. I want those pieces of paper that I told you about, and if I don't get them I'm stayin' right here, and if you're so fuckin' sure I ain't got nobody in here, then call my bluff and find out. But only two ways I leave here. With them papers, or dead with another dead man next to me."

"Stick." Another voice, and I recognize it.

"Who's that?" He's surprised to hear someone call him Stick.

"It's Crunch, Stick. You really fucked yourself this time, man."

The pace seems to be quickening. Everyone's talking.

The Stick makes that snorting half-laugh again. "Man, they got *all* the heavyweights out there, don't they?"

"Stick, you ain't got a chance, brother. You should see this place out here. It looks like Vietnam, man. You gotta come out. They got you. There just ain't no other way."

"They? They got me? You mean you ain't one of 'em no more? There's black pigs, too, and you is the biggest nigger motherfuckin' pig of 'em all."

"Stick, that ain't gonna do you no good, callin' names. I told you it's like a battlefield out here, and there's people out here gettin' tired and they're late for dinner, you know what I mean? And they're beginnin' to think the best way is to blow that elevator away and wrap the whole thing up and get on home. You see what I mean?"

"But you're talkin' 'em out of it, right, Crunch? 'Cause you're my friend. All I got to do is listen to my friend and come on out and everything'll be all right. Man, Crunch, that shit stopped workin' with me when I was seven. Who you think you talkin' to?"

"Have it your way, Stick. You're a dead man."

[BLACKSTONE 6]

We go through the mother bit and she's in tears, just about hysterical when it's over, and of course it didn't accomplish anything except maybe make the Stick even meaner than he was.

D'Angelo starts again about shooting it out. "This is a lot of bullshit," he says. "Let's stop fucking around with this clown and take him out of there."

Then Hanson gets sore and tells D'Angelo to shut up. In front of everyone. And D'Angelo gets red and turns on Hanson and tells him to keep his mouth shut, that this is a place for cops, not booksmart college paper shufflers. And you could see that hit, that tore right in among the nerves. So Hanson shut up and D'Angelo went on some more about opening the doors. And around this time I start wondering where the PC is. He should be here by now.

Then Perna gets on the intercom and tries to bullshit the Stick, and then he tells me, "You know him, you talk to him."

Well, I didn't have any bright ideas to offer, so I wasn't too ready to knock anything. I give the Stick the old buddy-of-mine routine, and he laughs in our faces, for which I can't blame him, like we're insulting him.

[LOCKLEY 11]

I believe what Crunch says about the battlefield—I *know* that's true—and I almost half believe about the guys who want to blow the elevator away and get home to dinner. I know there are men out there with that mentality—"Look, maybe there's no one in there at all. Let's just bring it up, open the doors, and blast him." You know.

So now it's around six o'clock, and things are getting really bad. I haven't had anything to drink since some beers in White's around noon, and I'm dying of thirst. I haven't eaten since breakfast at about eight-thirty. But the worst is the heat and the stink. I've managed to get my shirt off and bunched up and I'm sitting on it, because my ass is about to break from that floor. And I'm pouring sweat and so is the Stick. He's as bad off as I am, keeps licking his lips, and wiping sweat off his face, and the wall by the intercom where he's been leaning is all wet and muddy with dirt and sweat, and there's sweat and mud all over the floor around where it's been dripping down our legs, and his shorts are soaked in sweat.

And it's hotter than hell, must have been over a hundred, and the air coming through those louvers you can hardly even feel when you put your hand up. And I look at him sitting there, the shape he's in, the miserable, hot, sweating, stinking, tired, desperate, scared shape he's in—and I think about Chiclet. If she could see him now! No charm now, no composure now. And I really wish I could talk to him. I'd like to talk to him about Chiclet, ask him a few questions. What's he really think about her? Is *he* thinking about her now? Maybe so. Who knows?

So now for hours there's nothing over the intercom, and we

just sit looking at each other, for hours, trying not to go to sleep. Just heat, and sweat, and stink, and my ass breaking, and cramps in my legs, and trying not to nod, and telling myself over and over, "One nod, Bo, and you're dead. One nod, Bo, and you're dead."

[BLACKSTONE 7]

Perna starts getting ideas. I think D'Angelo is getting to him. Perna doesn't say so, but I think he wants to try to precipitate something. He says, what if we turn out the lights in the elevator. I say that the Stick is a lot meaner and sharper than Lockley, and that Lockley might be a smart guy reasoning things out, that kind of smart, but this Stick is out of the street, and very clever, cunning. I mean, you take a heavy dealer like that, a young cat with a background like his, and he's gotta be sharp and mean. Lockley's no match for that. Anything we do to upset things in there, like turning off the lights, is gonna give an advantage to the Stick. The best we can do for Lockley is to keep everything the way it is, and let him try to think his way out if he can. But not rock the boat, not give the Stick a chance to get up on him. I climb up on my horse, and I say all that. And Perna stops talking about turning out the lights.

A while before this, the Otis man had said there's a trap door in the top of the elevator. And Hanson says maybe the Stick will try to come out through the trap door and climb up the shaft. Perna says to open all the outer elevator doors on the shaft and put men outside each door. They do that. And now you can see that the elevator is right between the floors, the top of it sticking up about four feet into the shaft above the level of the floor we're on. You can see the trap door the Otis man talked about, just a raised area in the middle of the top of the elevator.

Hanson says why not darken the floor and watch the elevator with snooperscopes, the infrared scopes, and then if the Stick looks up through the trap door he'll see darkness and maybe he'll come out, up on top of the elevator, and we'll be able to see him and maybe get a shot at him. Perna buys that and we get a guy from the store to get blankets and it takes about an hour to get them nailed up over all the windows, and to get a couple of scopes and an infrared projector set up. Emergency Service lugs up some of their lights, these floodlights for outdoors, four of them, and they rig them up outside the elevator, about twenty feet from the elevator, all of them aimed right at it, so if the Stick comes out of that elevator they can hit the switch and it'll be like daylight, double-daylight, only we'll still be in the dark, and the Stick won't be able to see anything, he'll be blinded.

We have some shotguns and Thompsons there, too, and an old Springfield .03 sniper's rifle with an infrared scope with a man from the range who's supposed to be the best shot on the force. And we're all ready.

[LOCKLEY 12]

So we're sitting there for hours, and then all of a sudden there's a jolt, and a noise outside the elevator, and we both jerk up, like ready for anything, scared. We don't move, and then the Stick says, he doesn't look at me, he says it to the intercom, he says, "Hey, pigs! I'll blow his ass off, you open that door. I'll blow his motherfuckin' ass off. I'm tellin' you, pigs, you're killin' him!"

I stick the piece out a couple of inches closer to his belly.

What they had done, they had just opened the outer door. The Stick moves his ass around on the floor, so he's sitting more facing the door. And he's *watching* that door. I am absolutely convinced that at that minute, if that door had so much as *vibrated,* he would have shot me. I'm convinced.

But nothing happens. No one says anything back on the intercom, and there aren't any more noises, and after a while we both settle down again into the sweat and the stink and the heat, and wait.

Then I've got to go to the bathroom. Ever since we came into the elevator, I've had to go, but not so bad, and I was thinking about other things. But since about six, since the conversation with Crunch, I've really had to go bad, and thinking about that keeps me awake, because I don't want to just let it go in my pants. I know the Stick must be having the same problem, but I want him to do it first. I don't want to be the first. And I keep myself awake a long time on that, thinking about this competition between us not to be the first one to piss.

And then I just can't, and I let go and my pants, which are soaked with sweat anyway, go all dark, and the Stick looks, and he doesn't say anything or give any kind of an expression, he just notices it, that's all. And he waits a few minutes longer,

164

like he hasn't been bothered at all, and he goes, all over his shorts and his legs and on the floor, and now the floor is a big puddle of sweat and piss and the whole place is steaming—actually steaming—in the heat. But it helped keep me awake. I'll say that. It helped keep me awake, all that stink.

[BLACKSTONE 8]

About thirty of us are sittin' around in the dark, in bullet-proof vests, hotter than a son of a bitch, and Perna and D'Angelo and a couple of uniformed men even have helmets on, and Perna is telling everyone to keep their helmets on, but in the dark and the heat a lot of the men put them on and then take them off.

I mean it's not just the heat, but the whole thing is a little, I don't know, not ridiculous really, but it looks like the Army, not like cops. Men in vests hiding behind counters and Perna giving orders like he's a general. And that elevator sitting over there in the dark, sticking up in the shaft.

It got real quiet, eerie, you know what I mean? Everyone sittin' around watching that black thing stickin' up in the shaft, just a black shape, a shadow, that you could hardly see when you weren't on the scope. You had to feel bad for Lockley. You knew how hot it was in there, and frankly at that time I didn't think he had a chance, not with the Stick. The Stick will wait in there and watch him, stalk him in there, like an animal, until Lockley does something wrong, until he just closes his eyes for a second or looks away, and that'll be it. I remember sitting there in the dark and the quiet, just people breathing around me, and I *knew* how it was gonna end. It was gonna end with a shot. In all that quiet, one neat shot. Lockley was gonna blink his eyes, the Stick was gonna grab for his gun, Lockley was gonna be dumb and fight, and the Stick was gonna put a bullet in him.

Then I start thinking about Lockley's father, that he should be here. And I go to Hanson and say why not get Lockley's father here, that he should be here, and he agrees and crawls over to the edge of the counter where Perna and D'Angelo are

166

sprawled out and he mentions it to them, and Perna doesn't even move or say anything, but D'Angelo says, "I think we've got enough sentiment around here already." Just that, and Hanson comes back. D'Angelo is still wanting to open fire and end the thing and he's trying to act like anyone who doesn't agree with that is soft.

We sit around for a couple of more hours or so, and then Crowley, the department press guy, comes up, stumbling through the dark, and finds Perna and wants to know what about the press. He says they're all crowded down on the first floor and they want up, especially the photographers and the TV men, and he says the network guys want to put a camera here on the floor and shoot it live for the 1 a.m. news.

I thought I'd shit. Live for the 1 a.m. news! That's all we need, man. And for a minute I think maybe Perna is gonna go for it. You know, he might just. Then he tells Crowley to forget it, and Crowley says, well someone's gotta talk to them anyway, can he just bring up a couple of photographers and a couple of reporters so they can get some pictures and have a fast look around, for everyone, a pool, you know.

Perna says okay. And they come up. Perna tells them more or less what the score is, but not everything, just that there's a suspected heroin dealer in the elevator and we think he's got a cop with him and that makes it hard to do anything because we're all very concerned about the safety of the cop.

But these reporters are cute, and one of them asks about the girl found shot to death in an apartment on 47th Street, and is there a connection between that and this. Perna says that that possibility is being investigated. The reporter says, well it was a girl who was shot, and people said they saw two men with guns running up Fifth Avenue, and it looks like these two men in the elevator are those two guys.

Perna repeats what he said, that it's being investigated. Then this reporter says, "Is there a chance that there's a romance angle to this thing, a love angle?"

Well, D'Angelo has just been standing there, listening, not saying anything. But that question wakes him up. He says, "A what?"

And the reporter says, "A love angle, between the girl and one of these men in the elevator."

And the other reporter adds on, "Or both."

And D'Angelo—you can see that brain in there whirrin' around. And he says, "We are investigating every possibility."

The reporter says, "Including the possibility of romantic connections?"

Perna glances at D'Angelo. D'Angelo hesitates for a second, and then he says, "Including everything."

The reporters are falling over themselves in the dark to get outa there. Perna doesn't show any reaction at all. He just looks at D'Angelo and walks away. D'Angelo grabs Hanson and takes him into the buyer's office, and they're lost in there for an hour.

[HANSON 6]

Very late that night two reporters came up to the floor and one of them asked Chief Perna about the possibility that there had been some romance, some kind of a triangle, between Butler and Lockley and the Stick. It was a ridiculous suggestion. I was waiting for Perna to knock it down, laugh at the reporter and tell him he was full of shit. But before he had a chance to say anything, D'Angelo interrupted. He said every possibility was being investigated, including that one. I expected Perna to come up behind that and kill it, but he didn't say anything. He just let D'Angelo's words hang there. And the reporters took off.

Another detective was listening to this, too—Richard Blackstone—and he must have seen the look on my face. He came up to me and he said, "What's he mean? What's he trying to say? What's he aiming at?"

I didn't say anything. I think we both knew what he was aiming at.

[BLACKSTONE 9]

I'm thinking where the *hell* is the PC? When is he gonna come and get some sense in all this? D'Angelo's edging up on Perna. Pushing him, and with a little more pressure Perna is gonna fold. If the PC was here, D'Angelo'd suggest opening up on the elevator, and he'd suggest it *once*. He wouldn't be leaning on the Commissioner the way he is on Perna. The PC wouldn't take it. And you *know* there wouldn't be none of this shit about romantic connections. No one would have the balls for that with the PC here. I was thinking that if the PC were here, it would hold things in, hold things in a lot.

[HANSON 7]

Almost immediately after the reporters left, D'Angelo pulled me into the buyer's office. He closed the door and he said, "That reporter had a great idea."

I said, "What are you talking about?"

He said, "*He* knows what happened. He knows what caused this whole thing. He knows who's to blame. It's obvious."

I said, "What do you mean?"

He said, "Let me tell you what happened. Butler came to us and wanted to get tight with the Stick, right?"

I nodded.

"She never said anything about liking the Stick or wanting to shack up with him or anything like that, right?"

He gave me a look, like a shrug, and I nodded again.

"But she got a little too emotionally involved. She got carried away with the Stick. After all, the Stick was very good-looking, very dynamic, glamorous, romantic. Butler was an active girl who liked danger and adventure. Then Lockley found her. He liked what he saw. He followed her, talked to her, maybe it was even love at first sight. He saw her with the Stick, and it made him mad. Then he hit the Stick's flat, saw her nude in his arms, and killed her. If Butler had obeyed orders, and if Lockley had been a little more mature and less impulsive, it wouldn't have happened. It was unfortunate. It was tragic. But it was unavoidable. Every precaution was taken."

D'Angelo was actually *smiling*. I didn't say anything. Then D'Angelo said it wouldn't be a bad idea if that version of the story got leaked to the papers before too much other rumoring and speculation could begin. He said he'd see to that. He said that it was quite clear the Stick would not survive the morning,

171

and if Lockley did, it would of course be necessary to book him for homicide.

He said he'd talk to Perna and arrange to have an ADA come up to the store so he'd be here if and when Lockley came out alive.

[BLACKSTONE 10]

D'Angelo and Hanson came out of the buyer's office, and Hanson looks like he's in shock. D'Angelo starts whispering around for the Otis man and asks him can he shut off the air going into the elevator, the ventilation, and the Otis man says yes.

I crawl over to Hanson, 'cause he's like the junior one, and the only one with any kind of sense at all, and I say, "Excuse me, sir," very polite. "Excuse me, sir, but isn't that going to hurt Lockley more than the Stick?" Because of what we'd talked about before, that anything like that, any boat-rocking, has to hurt Lockley.

Perna hears me and tells me to get back over to the scope. So I go back over to the scope. They argue for a while, and then Perna says no, don't shut the air off, and D'Angelo is furious.

You've got to understand about the heat. This is June, and it's *hot*. It's hot out where we are, and in that elevator it's got to be like an oven. If they turn off the air, it'll go up to way over a hundred in there. You wouldn't be able to live in there.

We sit and we wait. Two, three hours. Then someone comes back from the phone and says, "It was on the 1 a.m. news, they saw it on the 1 a.m. news, right after Johnny Carson." He says they had shots outside the building, floodlights, all the police cars and trucks. Perna nods his head and says, "Now just wait."

About three minutes later, someone calls Perna to the phone in the buyer's office and after about ten minutes he comes back and says something to D'Angelo and then sits, staring at the elevator.

Q: What time is it now?

173

A: I would say it's about 1:30 in the morning, something like that.

Q: Okay. Go ahead.

A: We sit there. And nothing happens. It was weird. Through the scope you can see the elevator clearly, like it was in daylight, only red-tinted. But without the scope, it's like I said, this black shape, this shadow, except for a little sliver of light under the trap door. And that light was the only thing that made you know something was in there. Otherwise, without that light, I think it would have been hard to believe, that there was anything there at all. Because no one had used the intercom for hours, and it was very quiet. It was unreal. I mean, this is a department store. Saks? And all these men sitting around on the floor in vests and helmets and all this gear, the guns, you know what I mean? Right there with all the men's clothes. It was weird.

I stared at that piece of light. I almost went blind staring at that piece of light, thinking what was behind it, down in there, Lockley, this ignorant Lockley, and the Stick. And out here, here I am. And Perna, and D'Angelo. I'd of given anything to put Perna or D'Angelo in there, instead of Lockley.

Let's see. Then about 3:30 in the morning they call Perna to the phone again, and when he comes back he rounds up the Otis man, and the Otis man disappears in the dark some place, and I know right away where he's going. He's going to shut off the air. And D'Angelo and Hanson, neither one, they don't say anything, don't even move, like they know, and that's that.

[LOCKLEY 13]

I'm watching my watch and wondering what's going to happen next. There's no sound from the intercom, and the Stick seems resigned to sit there till they make a move. Then, at about four in the morning, I stand up, just to stretch a little, and I put my hand up by the louvers and there's no breeze at all. I point at it to the Stick and he gets up and puts his hand there and he says, "The pigs have shut off the air. Your friends. They ain't bein' too nice to their pig buddy, are they?"

He starts talking then, first time all night. But talking slow and very low, kind of to himself, like in a dream, and I see what all of this has done to him, his reactions, the way he's behaving, and I figure it must have had the same effect on me. I think we were both in a daze by that time, in shock a little.

He says, "That's what they think of you. They *showed* you what they think of you. Shut off your air. Think that'll get me outa here."

He laughs, quiet and tired. "Man, that's funny," he says. "The Stick surrenders to get into the cool."

Then he looks up at me, groggy, his eyes drooping, but still with a good firm grip on the gun, and he licks his lips. "You notice somethin'? Somethin' about all this?"

I shake my head.

"You didn't notice it?"

I look at him.

"You didn't notice the them and us? It's them and us, man. They don't care *shit* for you, whoever you are. Look at you. Sittin' there in a puddle of piss and sweat, and in a while longer it'll be shit, too. Thirsty. Hungry. Gonna die any minute. And they don't care. Not a-*tall*."

He shakes his head and he's quiet and we just sit there, for maybe another half hour.

Then he says, "But *they* got a problem out there *we* ain't got. They ain't got the piss and the sweat, but they got their problem, too. What they gonna do?" He laughs. "Yeah, what they gonna do with us. With *us*. *Not just me, man. Us.* By now this has been in all the papers and the TV and the radio, and it's gotta be all over everywhere that these people is holed up in this elevator and won't come out, and they got Fifth Avenue out there all blocked off and the TV and papers is waitin' to see what happens. What they gonna *do?* Man, they gotta do *somethin'.* Before this mornin' is over, they got to do *somethin'.* And you wanna know somethin'? They're gonna stop worryin' about you. They *already* stopped worryin' about you. They're gonna blow up this elevator with you and me in it, and that'll solve their whole problem. That's the *only* thing that'll solve it. You think those old pig bosses out there is on your side? You ain't that dumb, is you? You know whose side those old pig motherfuckers is on? Their *own* side. They is them, and we is us. That's the way it is."

Well, my mind is a little cloudy at this point, but I'm half beginning to believe him. I know the pressure they're under out there, and I know it's going to get a lot worse during the morning, with the papers and the TV. I can see the mayor getting to the PC. It doesn't look right to be running a city like New York and have some guy in an elevator getting all that attention and making all that trouble just because he won't come out. They can't let that go on forever. They've got to get him out. They can't wait for him to starve. They can play it straight for a while, and then they've got to do something desperate. They've got to do *anything,* just to put an end to it. Right? So I had to admit to myself that it did look a little like them and us, as the Stick put it. Me and him inside, and the bosses outside.

So anyway, we sit. And we sweat. And we piss. Physically and mentally, we piss. And trying to stay awake, I'm thinking about what the Stick said. And then at 11:30 in the morning, I cough. Just a little cough. Then I cough again, and the Stick coughs. I think it's the stink and the heat—which now has to be about 130 or something—and even when my eyes start to water, I still think it's just the sweat in my eyes.

[BLACKSTONE 11]

Everyone's pretty tired now, and no one talks much. We watch that black shadow, and take turns at the scopes. They've got another marksman and the two of them are spelling each other, one of them sleeping on a couch in the buyer's office, and I think Perna went in there once or twice, too, to try to sleep, but he didn't stay long.

After a few more hours, at about seven or eight in the morning, I begin to think maybe Lockley's gonna make it. If nothing has happened yet, maybe the Stick's not that big a match for him as I thought.

Then, around nine, Perna starts getting calls. They're really going after him now. Everyone's getting up and they're hearing that the Stick's still here, and they're getting panicked. They're thinking, how long is this going to go on.

And it's getting to Perna. He's harassed. He looks like he's been through a war. And D'Angelo has this attitude all over him, like, "If you'd done what I said last night, it'd all be over now and there wouldn't be any problem."

At about eleven, Perna and D'Angelo get together, and then Perna tells the Emergency Service captain that he wants tear gas. They get a CN canister, and they get the Otis man, and it's very clear that this is it, now or never, it's all going to end.

Perna says they're going to shoot a little gas in through the ventilating ducts, and see what develops. Everyone gets ready. Lockley and the Stick can't stay in there once the gas goes in. Either the Stick gives up and comes out, or he tries to go up through the trap, or they shoot it out inside.

Perna has three men with Thompsons in a semicircle around the elevator, about thirty feet from it, just outside where the lights are, so when the lights come on, the guns'll be in the dark.

177

It's still very dark, with the blankets over the windows, and I try to think of what to do, what could I possibly do. I know this is the end now, and I don't want to be thinking fifteen minutes from now, when Lockley's splattered all over the store, that there was something I should have done.

[LOCKLEY 14]

Now the Stick rubs his eyes, and coughs, and looks around the elevator. With his piece on my belly, he looks around the elevator. Glancing, never taking his eyes off me. And then he swears, and very carefully, slowly, he takes my shirt off the floor and jams it up in the louvers. Then he sits down again.

"Your pigs," he says. "You believe me now, man? Them and us. They're worryin' a lot about you, man, ain't they."

"Henderson!" It's Chief Perna.

The Stick doesn't stand up. "Yeah, pig, we're here."

"You ready to come out?"

"What you puttin' that stuff in here for, man? Your pig buddy don't like it. He's got enough troubles with the sweat and the piss."

"Just a whiff, Henderson, to wake you up. But we've got more. We've got a lot of things out here, Henderson. Are you coming out or not?"

He doesn't answer. He sits there and he stares at me. Then he takes my shirt down and waves it around in the elevator, like a fan, and in a few minutes you can almost breathe again.

The Stick folds the shirt up into a square and holds it over the intercom. Then he whispers to me. He says, "Look, man, I'm not sure who you are or what you are, but I know you want to go on livin'. You know as well as me that they got to get us out of here and they is gonna do anything now that they has to. If they gave a shit for you, they wouldn't be puttin' no gas in here. And you heard him, they got more, and they got guns and no tellin' what all they got out there by this time. There's only one way you can get outa this, but we gotta cooperate with each other. You know what I'm talkin' about? We got to trust each other a little bit. You wanna hear it?"

I don't say anything. I just look at him. But I don't shake my head, I don't say no. I'll tell you. I'd had it. I couldn't stand much more, and I knew it. I knew it.

He's still holding the shirt on the intercom and he's got his gun on me, and he gestures with his head up at the ceiling. "You see them louvers up there? That's a trap door. You push it open, you can get up on top of this elevator. If I get up there in the shaft, maybe I can move around some, get to another floor. I'll take my chances. But you gotta come with me. I ain't gonna trust you to keep your mouth shut while I'm crawlin' around up there. You do it?"

I shake my head, no.

"Listen," he says, and he's not talking mean, he's talking very tired, and I don't know if he's sincere or if he just sounds that way because he's so beat. "Listen," he says, "you ain't lettin' me go if you do it. You know as well as I do I don't stand hardly no chance of gettin' out of this buildin'. Man, I ain't even got clothes on. I couldn't get outa this buildin' even if they wasn't lookin' for me. You ain't lettin' me go."

I don't shake my head. I don't do anything. I know it's a con, but sometimes a con can be true, right?

"You know it's the only way you're gonna get outa here. We stay, they gonna kill us both."

I nod my head, and stand up. He drops the shirt and reaches up and gives the louvers a push. They loosen. He looks at me, and he whispers, "We gotta trust now, man."

[BLACKSTONE 12]

I get this idea to be close, close to the elevator, that maybe if I'm right up there I'll be able to do something. I tell Perna that I want to go up alongside the edge of the elevator and if they come out the top, or if the Stick lets them open the doors, I can get a shot at him. Perna says, what about the Thompsons. I say, at the range they're at, that close, I'm not worried, and anyway if anything happens where they've got a shot at the Stick, there's more chance of my picking him off with a revolver from a couple of feet than of them doing it from twenty feet. Because if they open up they're gonna get the Stick all right, but they're also gonna stand a good chance of getting Lockley.

Perna says, okay, go ahead.

I talk to the men with the Thompsons, we have a nice friendly little chat, and I remind them again that it's the nigger they're after. They're maybe a little itchy and I don't want them opening up on Lockley. And then I crawl up to the elevator and get down, crouching down, on the edge, on the left, right next to it, and if the doors open I'll be able to get my arm in and maybe with the surprise and the lights I can get a shot off and smother the Stick before he does anything. And I'll have a good chance against him with my vest. If he comes out the top, I should be able to get him up there.

They turn on the gas. In about ten seconds I hear a cough inside. Three minutes more, and I hear the top coming up, the trap door, and I see these hands pushing it aside, a lot of light is coming up from inside, and I'm just waiting for a black head to come up in that light so I can blow it off.

[LOCKLEY 15]

Then for the first time since we'd been in there, the Stick takes his eyes off me and looks up. Then he puts both hands up, still with the gun in one hand, and he pushes on the louvers and the trap door lifts. He twists it around, and pushes it over to the side. He puts his hands together like he would give me a lift up.

I put my foot in his hands and reach up with one hand and grab the edge of the opening and try to keep the gun aimed at him. I don't know what he's planning, and I'm still trying to keep him covered. He boosts me up and I crawl through and I'm on top of the elevator.

Then he reaches up and grabs the edges and pulls himself up, and we're both standing there on top of the elevator in the shaft.

[BLACKSTONE 13]

I see shoulders coming up, and the back of a neck, and it's white, it's Lockley, and he's got his back to me. He's right there, I can almost touch him, and I can't do anything. He's looking back down into the elevator, and I've just about made up my mind to go for it, to grab him off of there, when up comes the Stick between us.

The Stick's got a gun in his hand, and I've got a gun aimed at the back of his head, four feet from the back of his head, and his gun must have been right in Lockley's belly, and I don't know what to do.

Then the Stick kicks the trap over the hole to cut out the light, and he turns halfway around and he's squinting, trying to see into the dark. I don't think he realized till then that the outer doors were open, and he's starting to realize real fast that if the doors are open, what kind of trouble he's in.

He crouches down and Lockley moves around him, toward my side, and is crouching down too, and they're side by side, and I decide to make my move. I'm going to grab for Lockley.

[LOCKLEY 16]

The Stick moves the trap door back over the hole, just leaving a little opening where some light can get through, not much, just barely enough so we can see each other. We're standing on top of the elevator with our guns, and the top is about three feet above the floor, so we crouch down and try to see into the store. And we're staring out into the blackness, squinting, trying to see something, and then—*lights,* all the lights in the world, like someone had shoved the sun in my face.

I throw myself up against the shaft wall. I don't know what's happening. Then guns fire. Machine guns. The Stick yells. I'm thinking, "They're shooting at *me,* at *me, why are they shooting at me?*" I must have gone out of my mind.

I'm blinded by all that light. The world sounds like it's coming apart, and I start shooting. I don't know why. I must have been crazy. And then I hear my name and someone grabs my legs and pulls me down on the floor of the store and the guns are still firing, automatic fire, and then I hear something else, like an explosion, cracking, and I'm on the floor covered with sparks and there's this enormous cracking and then crashing, and then the firing stops and I'm lying there on the floor just hearing voices and people yelling and moving, but no more firing.

Someone picks me up, and it's Crunch, and he and another man carry me through the aisle—I remember stacks of sweaters in cellophane bags—into a little room like an office and they help me down into a chair.

[BLACKSTONE 14]

Then the lights go on, and everything opens up. The Stick is hit, and I yell at Lockley, but I don't think he heard me. He was pasted up against the shaft wall like he wanted to go through it. And then he reaches one arm out and starts shooting back. You can't imagine what it was like. All that light, after all night in the dark, and the Thompsons all going at once—Lockley must have gone crazy then. I mean, it was enough to make me crazy, and after what he'd been through in the elevator . . .

I reach up and grab him and yank him down to the floor. Then the Thompsons cut through the cables, and the elevator goes. It cuts loose and drops, the Stick with it, and we're buried in sparks. Another detective comes up then, and we carry Lockley into the buyer's office. We can hardly lift him. He's covered with piss and sweat. I never saw anything like that. Never anything.

[LOCKLEY 17]

Crunch looks at me and he says, "You're a mess, Beauregard," and he's got that Crunch grin. Chief Perna comes in, and he says to Crunch and the other guy, "What's he say about Butler?"

Crunch says, "We just brought him in."

And the chief says, "Butler's dead."

"Who's Butler?" I say.

"Detective Butler," the chief says.

"I don't know any Detective Butler," I say.

Then Crunch says, "The girl. Chiclet."

And that's the last thing I remember.

TAPE ENDS

[BLACKSTONE 15]

Q: What kind of shape was he in?

A: We put him in a chair and he was limp. I had to hold him up in the chair. He was numb. He looked at me like he didn't know who I was. And then Perna told him about Butler, and he just looked at Perna, just empty, like a zombie, and said he didn't know who Butler was. And then I told him. I told him. I was the one who told him. And he just passed out.

[HANSON 8]

Q: And Chief Perna sent for an ADA?

A: Yes. The ADA, Paul Jackson, arrived about forty minutes later. Perna told D'Angelo to brief him, and D'Angelo and I took him in the buyer's office and briefed him on what was going on, who the Stick was, and Butler and Lockley. D'Angelo was happy as hell with Jackson. On the way into the buyer's office, he whispered to me, "Great. Jackson's a headhunter. He'll tie him up good."

D'Angelo told him about Lockley's familiarity with the SDS and Weathermen at N.Y.U. and Columbia and said he suspected a connection, and that he also suspected a romantic connection between Lockley and Butler and the Stick, and that it was his own private opinion that Lockley killed Butler out of jealousy. He put the whole thing in his head. Jackson had known Butler, and I must say he wasn't feeling too kindly toward the guy who'd killed her. He was very receptive to D'Angelo.

After the shooting was over and Lockley was in the buyer's office and had come to and settled down a bit, Jackson took his statement. Lockley looked like he was in a daze. Physically, he was a wreck. His clothes were soaked, and if you got within ten feet of him you couldn't stand the stink. He looked to me like he was just coasting along on adrenalin. A department surgeon asked Jackson if he wanted him to give Lockley a shot of something, he meant to juice him up a little, keep him from passing out again. Jackson said, "Are you kidding? You go near him with a needle and I'll lock you up." Then he took the statement.

TAPE ENDS

ADA STATEMENT

Following is a statement taken from Det. Bo Lockley by ADA Jackson, June 10, 1971, commencing 12:30 p.m., ending 1:10 p.m., at Saks department store, New York, N.Y.

PRESENT: ADA Paul Jackson
                Asst. Ch. Insp. H. Perna
                Capt. J. D'Angelo
                Lt. P. Hanson

                Det. B. Lockley

Q: My name is Paul Jackson. I am an assistant district attorney. What is your name?

A: Bo Lockley.

Q: What is your address?

A: 298 Billings Place, Massapequa, Long Island.

Q: What is your occupation?

A: Police officer.

Q: What is your position in the Police Department?

A: Detective third grade. Sixteenth squad.

Q: Before we go any further, you know, do you not, that you do not have to answer any of my questions, and that you are entitled to have a lawyer, and confer with your lawyer, and that if you do not have money for a lawyer, a lawyer will be secured for you. And that if you answer my questions, anything you say may be used against you. Do you understand that?

A: Yes.

Q: Do you wish to answer my questions?

A: Yes.

Q: Did there come a time on June 9, which was yesterday, when you had occasion to fire your revolver?

A: Yes.

Q: Tell me about that.

A: I went into an apartment and there was someone there with a gun and I fired.

Q: Where was the apartment?

A: Forty-seventh Street between Sixth and Seventh.

Q: Who was in the apartment when you went in?

A: A man called the Stick and a girl called Chiclet.

Q: Who, if you know, is the Stick and who is Chiclet?

190

A: The Stick, I don't know, was just some guy, a junk dealer or someone, and Chiclet was a girl, a runaway, that I was looking for. Only now someone said her name was something else.

Q: You were looking for her and you found her, is that right?

A: That's right.

Q: When did you find her?

A: Last night. Two nights ago.

Q: How did you find her?

A: Someone told me she was with the Stick and where the Stick lived and I went there and I saw her and then I saw her again in a bar and I followed her.

Q: When was the first time you saw her?

A: On the street, a few weeks ago.

Q: When was the next time you saw her?

A: Two nights ago.

Q: You never saw her between those two times?

A: No.

Q: What was your reaction the first time you saw her?

A: I thought she was nice-looking. I felt sorry for her. I thought she was a junkie, a runaway and a junkie, and I felt sorry for her.

Q: Just sorry.

A: Right.

Q: What was your reaction when you saw her two nights ago?

A: The same. She was nice-looking.

Q: Just nice-looking?

A: She was very attractive. I think anyone would have thought that. She was very pretty and she had a very nice, a very attractive way about her.

Q: You said she was a runaway, you thought, and you were looking for her.

A: Yes.

Q: What did you do when you found her?

A: I followed her. I called Lieutenant Seidensticker. I made a date to meet her the next day.

Q: You made a date with her.

A: She said she'd meet me at this bar. She said if I kept following her, the Stick would get mad, get jealous or something.

Q: Did she keep the date?

A: No.

Q: How did that make you feel?

A: Worried. And mad. No one likes to be stood up.

Q: Did it make you jealous?

A: Of whom?

Q: Anyone. The Stick.

A: Maybe.

Q: What did you do?

A: I went to her apartment. His apartment.

Q: Did you expect to find them there together?

A: I guess so. Maybe so. I don't know.

Q: How were you feeling then, when you were going to the apartment? Were you mad, or jealous?

A: No one likes to be stood up. Also I was worried that maybe she was in trouble.

Q: What did you think of the Stick?

A: That he was a dangerous guy.

Q: How did you feel about his being with her?

A: I guess I didn't like it.

Q: Why?

A: She seemed too straight, too honest. He looked smooth, and slick.

Q: Did you think she'd be better off with you?

A: Yes, I thought that. I still think that.

Q: Were you mad at him for having her, jealous of him?

A: I think I was more mad at her. For giving herself to him, to someone like him.

Q: How mad were you?

A: Disgusted. I was confused. I didn't understand it.

Q: What happened when you got to the apartment?

A: I heard them in the apartment, and I went in.

Q: Were you mad then? At her or the Stick?

A: I don't know. Maybe.

Q: Did you go in because you were mad, or jealous?

A: Maybe. I said I don't know.

Q: Was it because you were mad or jealous or maybe just envious that you fired at them, or at either of them?

A: I don't think so.

Q: You're not sure?

192

A: I'm not sure of very much.

Q: Are you sure the Stick fired first?

A: I don't know what I'm sure of.

Q: Well, what happened?

A: I went in and they were there and I fired and he fired.

Q: Did you fire first?

A: I don't know. I don't remember.

Q: Is it possible you fired first?

A: I don't remember. It's possible. Anything is possible.

Q: Is it possible that you were angry and jealous when you went into the apartment, and that you saw them together nude and that when you saw them like that you became enraged and fired at them and killed her?

A: Anything is possible.

Q: Why did you enter the apartment?

A: I told you. She was there. So I went in.

Q: Did you know he was there with her?

A: I told you I heard him there. I heard them both. I was outside in the hall.

Q: What did you hear?

A: Talking.

Q: What happened when you fired?

A: He ran and I chased him.

Q: Then what happened?

A: We ran into the elevator.

Q: And you stayed in the elevator until—

A: The tear gas, the next morning, this morning.

Q: What happened then?

A: They put in gas, so we came out.

Q: Why didn't you come out before that?

A: He had a gun on me. I had a gun on him. We couldn't move.

Q: But when they put the gas in, you moved.

A: We had to move. It was us and them.

Q: What do you mean, us and them?

A: They were going to gas us, or blast us, if we didn't come out.

Q: What made you think that?

A: We figured it out.

Q: Who figured it out?

A: We did.

Q: Who's we?

A: The Stick and me.

Q: Who figured it out first?

A: The Stick.

Q: What did he say?

A: That they put in the gas, and they would blast us out, and our only hope was to cooperate and go out the trap door.

Q: So you cooperated?

A: If you want to call it that.

Q: How did you cooperate?

A: We cooperated by not killing each other.

Q: You came out first, up through the trap door. Is that correct?

A: Yes.

Q: How did you know he wouldn't shoot you when you got up in the trap door?

A: I just didn't think he would. It was part of how I felt.

Q: Part of the cooperation?

A: If you want to say that.

Q: Would *you* say that?

A: Yes, I'd say that.

Q: When did this cooperation start?

A: When the gas came in.

Q: Not before that?

A: No.

Q: Had you ever seen the Stick before this incident?

A: The first time I saw him was the night before.

Q: Never prior to that?

A: Not that I know of.

Q: Did you ever see him at Columbia, or N.Y.U.?

A: Not that I remember.

Q: At any SDS or Weathermen meetings, or any other meetings?

A: Not that I remember.

Q: There are a number of things that you don't remember.

A: I guess there are.

Q: Is it possible you did see him before, at Columbia or some of those meetings?

A: It's possible. I don't remember seeing him.

194

Q: Now, when you came up on top of the elevator, up through that trap door, you were standing on top of the elevator?

A: That's right.

Q: And Henderson, the Stick, came up after you?

A: That's right.

Q: And then the police officers, the other officers, started shooting?

A: That's right.

Q: And what did you do then, when they started shooting?

A: I started shooting, too.

Q: Why?

A: Someone was shooting at me. There were a lot of lights. I didn't know what was happening. I still don't know what's happening.

Q: You don't know what's happening now?

A: Not exactly.

Q: Do you know where you are?

A: Yes.

Q: Where are you?

A: Saks department store.

Q: Do you know who I am?

A: Yes. You're an assistant DA. That's what you said.

Q: Do you know what a Miranda warning is?

A: Of course.

Q: Do you remember my giving you the warning?

A: Yes.

Q: Well, I'll restate it now if you can't remember it. I want to be sure you remember it.

A: I remember it.

Q: Do you want a lawyer now, or do you want to stop answering my questions now?

A: No.

Q: So when you said you still don't know what's happening, that was a rhetorical statement, a figure of speech, rather than an accurate statement of fact?

A: That's right. I know what's happening.

Q: I had asked you why you started shooting.

A: Because of the lights, and I was confused. I was very hot, and tired, and I was cramped, and I was confused, and all

195

of a sudden there was all this light in my face, and guns going off all around me, and I guess I just went a little crazy.

Q: Did you think the police officers were firing at you?

A: I don't know. I guess I must have assumed they were. At me and the Stick. We were right next to each other. I don't know who else they could have been firing at.

[BLACKSTONE 16]

Q: Why do you think all of this happened?

A: All of it? I couldn't say. But Bo? Bo got hurt by animals he didn't even know were in the jungle. He was too nice. It was just a matter of time until he became somebody's victim. And I don't just mean the Stick. You understand? Bo and the Stick had more in common than you'd think. Very sharp kids. In different ways, but sharp, both of them. As much as I can say bad about the Stick, I could never say he was dumb. He knew the streets, he knew the people, he knew how to move. He knew what makes it all go 'round. Ordinarily, he and Bo wouldn't have been together five minutes. Maybe in a station house, but never in any kind of a situation where they were more or less on an equal basis—like with the same problem, sharing the same problem, how to get out of that elevator alive. And really forced to get to know each other. I mean if you're in an elevator with someone for twenty-two hours, sitting around in each other's sweat and piss, and ready to kill each other and figuring you're both gonna get blasted to hell just about any second, you're gonna get to *know* each other. Just watching the guy, looking at his face, the way he carries his fear, you know what I mean? Think about it, what it did to Bo, not just the physical thing or what happened in the elevator and the shooting, but what it did to his head. He had a long, *long* education that night. You should have seen him when he came out of that elevator. He was dazed, stunned. And filthy, covered with sweat and piss and stinking like a corpse. Right then I'd of sure liked to get inside his head and walk around and check out the sights.

Q: Was that the last time you saw him?

A: No. I was with him all that day. I went when they took him to Bellevue, and then the doctors didn't want to let him

197

go to court so I stayed around till about five o'clock when they arraigned him there in the prison ward. His father was there. That was some sad sight.

Q: Did you talk to him?

A: It was the first time I'd seen him in over ten years. We walked out of the hospital together. I told him I'd known Bo better than anyone else in the squad and did he want to have dinner. He said he'd meet me the next night in this Italian restaurant he knew on Queens Boulevard. So I went, and when I got there he was already at the bar. It was near the 112th squad and I recognized a couple of other detectives at the bar, but Lockley was drinking alone. We had a drink at the bar and then we sat down at a table. We were just talking, you know, about lots of things, about the 23rd when we were there together, but not about Bo, like neither of us wanted to bring it up. And the owner came over and Lockley introduced us, an old white-haired Italian, a nice guy. Lockley seemed to know him pretty well. And the owner—Carlo, his name was Carlo —was telling me how long he'd known Lockley and how all the cops from the one-twelve came in, and how they're the greatest guys in the world. And while he was talking, there were these two uniformed cops in one of the booths by the door and one of them kept staring at Lockley. He was a young kid with a skinny little pointed face like a rat, and a mustache hanging over his lip, and he was staring and whispering to his partner— like, you know, telling him, "Hey, there's Lockley, the guy whose son just got locked up."

And Lockley was talking to Carlo and trying not to notice. Carlo said what nice guys all the one-twelve cops were, and then he nodded toward the two in the booth and he said, "Only today, I don't know about it, some of them, it's like they want to take advantage. These guys in the radio car, they live in this place. Last week one of them, the guy with the mustache, he brings his whole family in here, his mother, his father, his brother, his sister, six people, and when I give him a check he's all upset about it. And tonight he comes in with his partner, and I say, I tell him, 'Look, I got to be careful. The IAD's been in here. They're watchin' me. I don't want no suspension, you know what I mean?' And he tells me, just before you came in, he says, 'Well, bring us the check and we'll give you a twenty and then bring back like four fives for change, and that way no one will know we didn't pay the check.' "

Carlo looked at Lockley and me and shrugged. "I mean, I like a cop, these fellas from the one-twelve, they all come in here, they're all my friends. I go to their house, they come to my house. But these new fellas, like these guys here in the radio car, they take advantage, you know what I mean . . ."

He left then and Lockley said to me, from nowhere, just after a couple of seconds' silence, he said, "Thanks."

I said, "For what?" But I knew for what.

"The elevator. He'd be dead now."

"Forget it."

We sat there for a while, and then I asked him, "Did you talk to Jackson?"

"Yeah. He didn't want to talk. He says he'll try to get it to the Grand Jury as soon as possible, next month. He thinks he'll have an indictment by the fifteenth. He's asking for Murder I."

"Jackson's a scum bag."

Lockley didn't say anything, just shrugged, like he didn't want to sound like he was asking for my sympathy.

"Why Murder I?" I said.

"Why not? What's he got to lose? He can always come down. He'll say Bo had plenty of time after he saw the two of them to think about what he was doing. He'll say Bo saw them and decided to kill her. Murder I."

I said, "Sylvester's a good lawyer." I'd seen him at the arraignment.

"Yeah. We'll see what he can do with Jackson."

"Bail?"

"Sylvester's going to ask for ten thousand. Jackson will ask for no bail. If we get twenty, twenty-five, we'll be lucky. More than that—"

I started to say, "The house?" Because I knew he lived out in Massapequa. But I didn't. Why the hell should I make him admit to me he's got his house in hock.

Carlo came back. "How's the dinner? You enjoy the dinner?"

Lockley smiled a big smile, and said, "Great, Carlo. Like always."

Rat-face was staring again. Carlo left and Lockley said to

199

me, "Ten years ago you saw a germ like that in uniform you'd give him a collar for impersonating a police officer."

We got up and said goodbye to Carlo and on the way out Rat-face was really giving Lockley a once-over, and Lockley stopped at his booth. I thought maybe he was going to do something stupid. But he just stopped there, and he looked down at the guy and he gave him a good hard East Harlem shot with those ball-bearing eyes and said, "Was there something you wanted to ask me?"

And Rat-face looked down into his spaghetti like he wanted to get under it and said, "No, sir."

So we left.

TAPE ENDS

PERNA
D'ANGELO
SEIDENSTICKER

Chief Perna and Lieutenant Seidensticker were interviewed in the IAD office and in every way supported and confirmed the versions given by other principals. Captain D'Angelo arrived at the IAD office with an attorney, and on advice of counsel refused to answer questions.

PSYCHIATRIC
EVALUATION

Detective Lockley was indicted for first-degree murder and held in $50,000 bail. On July 10 he was moved from Bellevue to the Tombs. After two weeks at the Tombs, he was placed in a mental-observation cell, where he was routinely examined by Dr. Stephen Oster, a psychiatrist employed part-time by the Dept. of Correction. Dr. Oster's evaluation follows.

PSYCHIATRIC EVALUATION
ON OBSO ADMISSION

Bo Lockley (9L301)

HISTORY: Lockley was placed in the OBSO section Thursday night after a fight on the fifth floor with another inmate who Lockley said tried to enter his cell just prior to evening lock-in. Lockley told Capt. Tullin that the other inmate, Frank Rutherford, a black, had been "making passes" at him all day and had said, "We know you're a pig and we're gonna make you eat every dick in the section." Lockley said Rutherford threatened to stick him with a homemade weapon (a sharpened bedspring was later recovered from the toilet bowl in Rutherford's cell) if he did not allow him to lock-in with him. Lockley told Capt. Tullin that he made no reply to these threats, but when Rutherford did attempt to lock-in with him he attacked Rutherford with his fists. Lockley admitted that to attract the attention of guards and to prevent Rutherford locking in with him, he deliberately held Rutherford's arm in the path of the closing cell gate. Rutherford was transferred to Bellevue for treatment of a fractured arm. Other inmates questioned said Lockley "started screaming and shouting and just went berserk."

MENTAL STATUS: Lockley is interviewed in his cell, Eight-Lower-A-Six (OBSO). He is wearing undershorts, sitting on bunk. When I approach he stands up. He is unshaven. Hair, which he wears long, is uncombed. Effect is flat, detached, yet anxiety is shown in constant pacing and nail-biting as we talk. Thinking is quick and perceptive. There appears to be obsessive thinking about responsibility and guilt. Asked the reason for his incarceration, he states, "I killed a girl. And a guy got killed,

204

too, because of me." Asked about his job as a police officer, he states, "I let my old man down. I let my brother down. I let the job down." Asked what he has been doing in jail, he replies, "I think. I sit and I think." About what? "Chiclet. My father. The newspapers. Jackson. My lawyer." Anything else? "How it happened. That maybe it's all true. That maybe I did fire at the Stick and at Chiclet out of jealousy. That maybe I did murder Chiclet. That maybe I should have been taken on a fishing trip." Asked what he means by "fishing trip," he ignores the question and states, "What am I doing here anyway, walking around on this planet?" There is no evidence of psychosis. He denies hallucinations. Mildly delusional. Serial 7 subtractions from 100 are done rapidly. Eight digits are repeated forward, six backwards. Orientation and memory intact. General information excellent. Pairs of abstract words are differentiated. Proverbs can be interpreted. There are fears of falling, and he has many recent nightmares he cannot remember.

IMPRESSION: Personality disorder—acute stress reaction. If left untreated and in present setting, permanent damage will almost certainly occur. Inmate is in immediate need of psychiatric therapy in a supportive, loosely structured setting. It would be difficult to imagine a more dangerous environment for this man than the one he is now in.

After interviewing Lockley and examining his file, it appears that he is a highly intelligent, adequately adjusted young man suddenly and severely torn by brutalizing events (or, rather, brutalizing people). In the confused aftermath of this ordeal, he is compelled to consider whether he was its cause, its catalyst, or merely a hapless passer-by. He finds himself pressed between two alternatives: rejection ("Nothing was my fault") and acceptance ("I am responsible"). It is not surprising that he selected the latter and reacted with guilt and a nearly intolerable conviction of responsibility. This man is bearing a dangerous burden. Unless swiftly relieved through intensive psychotherapy and change of setting, he may experience irreversible emotional impairment.

OBSO REPORT

Two days after the preceding evaluation, and at the time
portions of this report were receiving attention at the
district attorney's office with a view to dismissal of the
homicide charges, Detective Lockley hanged himself at
the Tombs. Following is an observation report kept on
Lockley the day of his suicide.

THE CITY OF NEW YORK
DEPARTMENT OF CORRECTION

DATE 7-11-71

INMATE B. Lockley. CHARGE Murder LOCATION 8LA6

Under Special Observation
Correction Officer's Report — Every 30 Minutes

8:00 A. M.	Refuse Breakfast
8:30 " "	Walking
9:00 " "	Walking
9:30 " "	Walking
10:00 " "	Sitting
10:30 " "	Walking
11:00 " "	Walking
11:30 " "	Walking
12 NOON	Refuse lunch
12:30 P. M.	Walking
1:00 " "	Walking
1:30 " "	Walking

2:00 " "   At 1:55 PM inmate XXXX B. Lockley (9L301) was found
2:30 " "   hanging in his cell from a noose fashioned from a
      torn bedsheet. I immediately called to the bridge and
      administered mouth to mouth resuscitation. Capt. Russo
3:00 " "   responded immediately with a resuscitator and attempted
      to revive the inmate. Dr. Rutherford responded and
3:30 " "   pronounced the inmate dead. Asst. Dep. Wrdn. Dunlop
4:00 " "   present. Warden notified. Death of Inmate Report
      filed. Unusual Occurrence Report filed. Command
   Relieved   Notification Report Filed. Body to Bellevue.

REMARKS ....

COR. OFFICER M. B.

CAPTAIN